I MUST TELL YOU

TIBOR ZAK

Order this book online at www.trafford.com
or email orders@trafford.com

Most Trafford titles are also available at major online book retailers.

Printed in the United States of America.

ISBN: 978-1-4907-4772-9 (sc)
ISBN: 978-1-4907-4771-2 (hc)
ISBN: 978-1-4907-4770-5 (e)

Library of Congress Control Number: 2014917832

Trafford rev. 10/08/2014

www.trafford.com
North America & international
toll-free: 1 888 232 4444 (USA & Canada)
fax: 812 355 4082

Contents

Hungary during World War II

During World War II, Hungary was a member of the Axis powers. In the 1930s, the Kingdom of Hungary relied on increased trade with Fascist Italy and National Socialist Germany to pull itself out of the Great Depression. By 1938, Hungarian politics and foreign policy had become increasingly pro-Italian and pro-German. Hungary benefited territorially from its relationship with the Axis. Settlements were negotiated regarding territorial disputes with the Czechoslovak Republic, the Slovak Republic, and the Kingdom of Romania. In 1940, under pressure from Germany, Hungary joined the Axis. Although initially hoping to avoid direct involvement in the war, Hungary's participation soon became inevitable. In 1941, Hungarian forces participated in the invasion of Yugoslavia and the invasion of the Soviet Union.

While waging war against the Soviet Union, Hungary engaged in secret peace negotiations with the United States and the United Kingdom. Hitler discovered this betrayal and, in March 1944, German forces occupied Hungary. When Soviet forces began threatening Hungary, an armistice was signed between Hungary and the USSR by Regent Miklos Horthy. Soon after, Horthy's son was kidnapped by German commandos and Horthy was forced to revoke the armistice. The regent was then deposed from power, while Hungarian fascist leader Ferenc Szalasi established a new government with German backing. In 1945, Hungarian and German forces in Hungary were defeated by invading Soviet armies.

Approximately three hundred thousand Hungarian soldiers and eighty thousand civilians died during World War II and many cities were damaged, most notably the capital of Budapest. Most Jews in Hungary were protected from deportation to German extermination camps for the first few years of the war. However, from the start of German occupation in 1944, Jews and Roma were deported to the Auschwitz Birkenau concentration and extermination camps. By the end of the war, the death toll was between 450,000 and 606,000 Hungarian Jews and an estimated twenty-eight thousand Hungarian Roma. Hungary's borders were returned to their pre-1938 status after its surrender.

Introduction

Imagine a wheelbarrow full of marbles and spilling all of them in your backyard, and then you have to sort them all by color using only a soup spoon. This is how I felt when I started this book, substituting my stories for the marbles and my memories for the soup spoon. Right now I am ninety years old.

I do not intend to bore you with an autobiography. It is true, however, that in many of the stories I am the main character. It is also true that many of the stories were told to me by relatives and close friends, but in either case the stories are shaped more by the circumstances. Because of my age, most of my contemporaries have passed away. But just to be on the safe side, I avoid names, recognizable locations, and dates to protect all.

The book covers twenty-two years of my life, fifteen to thirty-seven. I was thirty-five years old when we—my wife and two sons—left Budapest during the Hungarian Revolution, and went to the United States.

During my life, I attended hundreds of social events. Because of my accent people asked me where I came from, what I did, how it was living under communist dictatorship, etc. And the conclusion was many times: you should write a book; thus, the origin of the title, "I Must Tell You."

Starting out my name is not that simple. I was born with the last name of Jager, which is a German name since my ancestors came from Austria to Hungary. When I finished high school, I went to Germany for college and did not want possible pressure to join in the Nazi organization, so I changed my name to Zsak which was a Hungarian name. Consequently, all my college documents used Zsak. When arriving in the United States, all my immigration papers used the name Zsak.

The Zs in the name became a problem. People could not pronounce it, so they just avoided calling me by my name and just, "you." One day, months before we applied for citizenship, a kid knocked on the door, selling something. Looking over his note, he asked my last name. I said Zsak. He said it was a "goofy" name. As a result of this one kid, we changed our name to Zak.

The Summer of 1939

It was early evening. My father just returned home from work and was sitting down with a glass of wine. He said he had been thinking about my wish, to start my summer vacation by going to Germany for two weeks. He still thought that at age sixteen, I was too young, but he was closer to giving me the green light for two reasons. First, my mother died a year ago and she was always pushing me for self-reliance. Second, for the past two years I had really pushed him to let my learn gliding. He never agreed. I asked him what I could do to convince him that I was mature enough to travel alone. He said I should give him a written, day-to-day plan, and what I intend to do during the two weeks of vacation.

I was really surprised at the tone of the discussion since my godmother just days ago told me she could not convince my father to let me go.

I was sixteen years old, spoke fluent German, and had spent the last three Christmas in Kitzbuhel, Austria skiing. Admittedly these three trips were spent visiting my uncle and each trip lasted only nine days.

The beginning of the vacation was already full, first with Boy Scout camp, then with tennis tournaments. My planning focused on the end of August. The trip originated on the German railroad special offer to foreign students, ages fourteen to eighteen, to travel freely for two weeks for a very low price. The freedom to go any place with the pass, without restriction, was an insurance to cover a large area in a short time. The trip was further enhanced since there was a chain of guesthouses available to stay overnight, including breakfast for the price of a song. There was a guesthouse in practically every town for students sixteen years and over. For both boys and girls. Thinking back, the political climate was dangerous for an enjoyable vacation away from home. But who thinks about such things when you are sixteen years old.

To get the railroad ticket, membership for the guesthouses organization, planning, and investigating the route, etc., took all my time for two months. After presenting all my information to my father, we agreed that the last two weeks of August would be the best time to go.

Finally, I left Budapest on Monday, twenty-first of August. All of my belongings were placed in two bags. One was a small backpack, holding all my clothes and the other was a side pack. Both were brand new as were my walking shoes, although I had worn them for two weeks before the trip to break them in. I had two Boy Scout shirts with me, which were practical because they had pockets that I could use to keep my passport and money in.

The route began in Vienna, and then travelled through Southern Germany and Austria (which at that time was already part of Germany) and returned via Vienna to Budapest. The whole trip was a zigzag route of the Alps since I was more interested in the scenery than the large cities.

After three or four days I was bored following the route because I spent my time visiting old churches and museums, and looking at store windows without any reason to buy anything. I arrived in Garmisch on the sixth day of the trip on the twenty-sixth of August.

Garmisch was a picturesque Alpine city, home of the 1938 winter Olympics. The guesthouse was close to the railroad station. It was a two-story building, bright blue, with a large covered porch and lots of bicycles. It was early in the afternoon and there were few people outside. By the entrance, inside was a small office with a middle-aged lady attending the office. I asked her if she had a place for me and that I intended to stay for three to four days. She commented on my German name and told me that there was another Hungarian staying there. She said his name was Fritz, and that he was out but usually returned in the afternoon. I asked how old he was and she said he was eighteen and had been there for about a week.

I took my bags and looked up my assigned bed. It was upstairs by the wall in a large room. There were more than one hundred beds, closely lined up. On the same floor there was a large shower room with fifteen or twenty showers and many sinks. The hallway between the showers in the bedroom had a rope stretched from one side to the other for drying clothing. I did my laundry, organized my backpack, and went downstairs. The layout was the same as the upstairs except it has a large dining room with benches. The downstairs were for girls.

I left the guesthouse to get familiar with the city. I intended to buy a Tyrolian felt hat that most of the boys were wearing. The main purpose of the hat was to display colorful small emblems from all the tourist locations the person visited. I located one and purchased a gray hat, and also an emblem of Garmisch. A priority was to locate the bakery and a butcher shop since they were the places that would provide me with all my meals during my trip. After eating a healthy dinner of two big sweet rolls with milk, I started looking for ski shops. All the ski equipment was years ahead of what I had in Hungary.

Back in the guest house, it took me no time to find Fritz. He was older than me, about the same height but much more athletic looking. He was with a group of boys and girls. Seeing me approaching (apparently the lady who registered me told him my name and appearance), he ran toward and began introducing me. After finishing his discussion with the group, he sat down with me on a bench and we started a long discussion to get to know each other.

He was an only child and his mother was a companion of a rich Hungarian aristocrat. He was born in Budapest and lived there his whole life. After finishing primary school, he became an apprentice at a famous jewelry store in Budapest. After finishing his apprenticeship, he studied to become a master jeweler. This was about a year ago and during that time he discovered a unique way to make a living. Learning about and being familiar with diamonds, he purchased a one carat flawless diamond from his jeweler boss. He took the diamond to Switzerland and sold it for Swiss francs. He then exchanged the Swiss francs for an undervalued Hungarian currency of the time called Pengo. He spent the profits traveling and sightseeing in Europe. In the past year he had already made four trips.

He was upset when he discovered how thrifty my travel plans were. I asked him what I could see in Austria on the way home and told him that I have to be home on the third of September for the start of school. This meant I had eight days left of my vacation. He said he would think about it, but in the short-term he was planning to climb to the top of the Zugspitze the next day. He said he was planning to go alone but it would be more fun if I would go with him. I had no idea what was involved and thought nothing of it, so I agreed to go with him.

The next morning we woke up early, packed warm clothing, and had breakfast. We told the office where we're going and the guy in the office said we were nuts and better use the cable car if we want to be back by night. We walked over to the bakery and butcher shop to pick up food and water and then started on our way to Zugspitze.

Zugspitze is Garmisch's tallest mountain at 9,564 feet. The map listed Garmisch at 2,295 feet high, so that meant we had to climb 7,269 feet to reach the top. Actually, the highest we could go was a restaurant which was below the summit.

The weather was perfect, sunny, and not a cloud in the sky. We reached the base of the mountain after a two-hour walk. The air was crystal clear and we could see the summit, so it looked like the whole climb would be picture perfect. We could see the end of the tree line followed by a rocky area to the top. It looked like an easy three- or four-hour climb. We started out at about 10:00 a.m. and it was early afternoon when we left the tree line.

Then the slope became steep and we had to stop every five or ten minutes to catch our breath. Climbing some more, we discovered that we were going to have to deal with a vertical rock wall. We had to go a good distance to the right to find a narrow spot in the rock that was not so steep. When we reached the narrow spot, there was still a two- or three-story climb ahead of us. At the top of the climb there was a steel rail, and people were looking over the railing watching us. As we started to climb, people were pointing and yelling to us, directing us toward a narrow crevasse in the rock. They threw down a belt and a rope and then pulled up our backpacks. I was pulled up first and then Fritz. It was cold up there.

An older couple helped us put some of our warm clothes on because our hands were numb from the rope and the cold. They got us into the restaurant and told the owner what was going on. They had dinner with us and paid for it. Then the owner sat down with us telling us that there was not a single room available in the adjacent hotel. He offered to let us sleep in his small warehouse which was heated, had a washroom with a shower, and had lots of lounge chairs. Blankets finished the accommodations and we were very happy with the place. There was loud music coming from the restaurant but we fell asleep as soon as our heads hit the pillows.

The next morning after breakfast they told us how to find a walking path back to Garmisch. We started out walking on a marked path through a glacier, then down a steep path to a valley with a swift creek. The whole valley was lush green and you couldn't find a more gorgeous place to live the rest of your life. Fritz thought up a plan on the way down as to what we could do for the next five or six days. He said we should leave Garmisch and go over to Switzerland and down to San Moritz. My budget became an obstacle because I had no money for the train to Switzerland; also they did not have the inexpensive guesthouses like Austria. As I was to learn, Fritz always had a solution. He said the Swiss were friendly sorts and would gladly pick up hitchhikers. We could ask people if we could stay in their house which was common in small towns. If that didn't work, we could ask to stay at the local church.

Arriving back at Garmisch, we looked on the map to see that San Moritz was about one hundred twenty miles away. Along the road there were many small towns, so it looked like our chances of finding lodging were good. I wrote a letter to my father giving him the details of the new trip. We washed our clothes, packed our bags, and were ready to go.

Early in the morning, we left the guest house. The Swiss border was halfway to our destination. It took us two days to get to the border, and our last ride was a beer truck. When the driver dropped us, he showed us a tall chimney on the Swiss side. We took a narrow path through a small forest, a large cornfield, and then onto a road which put us into a small town.

The problem was that it was a Swiss town. We had somehow bypassed the official border crossing. We had to go back to the border crossing and explain the whole story to the guards. They asked routine questions and then stamped our passports. The next day, we were lucky because a truck took us all the way to St. Moritz. We arrived there after lunch. It was thirty-first of August.

The first priority was finding a place to stay. We ran into a monk working next to a small chapel. He offered us his garage, which had a shower, but told us we had to be back before 9:00 p.m. We walked over to the city and decided to visit a nearby glacier next day.

The next day, we were having breakfast in a bakery when we we're told that Germany invaded Poland. We stayed in the bakery and listened to the radio, all thoughts of the glacier long forgotten. All kinds of new regulations were being listed in a continuous news stream, including restricting private cars from traveling on the road.

We were a long way from the German border, and I had to get to Germany in order to take the train home. It was the first of September and the German border was 130 miles away. It was raining, and the forecast was rain all the way to the border for the coming week. School started in a week, and my train ticket expired on the fifth of September.

We decided to start heading home right away. By nightfall we reached a guest house, still in Switzerland. We got a room and had dinner, then went back to the room to discuss how we could get to Garmisch as early as possible. There were rumors that the Swiss would close the borders, but we hoped that they would be more interested in keeping people out than preventing us from leaving.

The first part of our trip was through a beautiful valley called the Engandin, which wasn't so beautiful because we walked in rain with high winds for two days since there was no traffic. By the third day, traffic was back to normal and, in driving rain, a car stopped and picked us up.

The driver took us to his home. His wife and kids were friendly. They gave us their guest room along with a much needed huge dinner. The man of the house was a doctor, and he offered to drive us to the border the next day because it was his day off. We were back in Garmisch on the fourth of September.

The next day, Fritz and I exchanged addresses, and Fritz said he would be back in Budapest in two to three weeks. I went to the train station and arrived in Budapest on the sixth of September. My father received the letter I sent from St. Moritz on the day I got home. He had sent money to the Hungarian Embassy in Geneva, trying to catch up with me. Fritz arrived in early October. We met a number of times into the next year, but then lost touch.

Fast forward to September of 1945. World War II ended in Europe in May. Budapest was occupied by the Russians in January. Life in the city was starting to return to normal. We had electricity. We had a police force that was largely able to prevent confrontations with the Russian soldiers. Everybody was cleaning up. The window glasses in most apartments were shattered and they were replaced with cardboard or anything else that could be found.

I moved to Pest, which was the east side of Budapest, got married, and conducted a lucrative smuggling operation. Out of nowhere, Fritz showed up. In 1940, he joined the Air Force, became a pilot and moved up in the ranks to become an officer. He served on the Eastern front, flying reconnaissance for the German and Hungarian Army. The airports he flew out of were usually far from the front. By the time he joined the fight, the Russians were forcing the Germans to retreat. A small group of Hungarian airmen, flying six to ten twin-engine planes, were doing reconnaissance flights. Some days were busy, others were spent playing cards. On one of his flights he landed at a new airport, which was still in Russia. The Germans had just refinished the landing strip. The place still needed to be organized, and that required a week so there was no flying that week.

The airport was next to a mostly vacant town. To occupy his time, Fritz searched the empty homes for memorabilia.

As he was heading back to his base, he walked by many bombed and burned out German trucks and cars. There were all rusty and grown in with weeds. Apparently this happened when the Germans were still advancing. All the trucks were located in a wooded area.

Next day he went back; as he was searching, there was a half-ton truck with small empty ammunition boxes and under the boxes there were small sacks, all closed up with neatly wound copper wire. He had a hard time pulling one out. It was the size of a thick book, but very heavy. He ripped it open, it was full of gold coins. He tried to count them but there were too many.

Next day he went back. He took all the sacks out from the truck and hid them in a ditch covered with high weeds. The place was about a mile from the airport. His intention was to transfer the sacks in the back of his plane. Since the content of the sacks was different (feeling the content with his fingers), he didn't want to carry them back to the plane without knowing what was in every one of them.

The problem was not opening them but closing them again. The reason was whoever closed them had used some kind of fixture to bundle up the opening and to wrap wire around. Once opened you could not gather enough material together to have room to wrap the mouth shut with the wire. Before he went back to the airfield, he counted the sacks. It was twenty-seven total.

Back at the airport, he looked everywhere to find some containers to hold the contents of the sacks. There was nothing even close.

His plan was to carry the sacks close to the plane during the day. He judged the weight of each at around fifteen pounds. He hid the sacks close to the plane, then in the twilight went back and hide it under the floor, telling the other pilots that he was going back to the plane to connect something on his radio.

Before falling to sleep the same night, he figured out how to open and close the sacks. First, he had to unwind the wire and check the content then close the opening by holding the two sides of the sack flat to the ground, use the wire to go back and forth weaving the two sides shut.

The next day he tried it out and it worked. So for the next week he accomplished the transfer of twenty-seven sacks to the plane.

After many stops they flew back to Austria to a remote, small airport. The Germans had abandoned it and the Americans had not yet arrived. He had time to hide the gold in a twelve-foot deep ravine in the forest covered with thick bushes. Three hundred yards from the hole, he marked the spot by driving nails into five trees.

Back in Budapest, Fritz asked me to help him retrieve the gold, saying he would give me half. I asked him how long he thought it would take, and he said it could be a month, could be six months, depending on how much activity was in the area. I told him I was too involved with my own life to participate in another adventure.

In 1959, living and working in a Chicago suburb, I had lunch with colleagues one day. One of them said he read an interesting article about a sculptor who left Hungary the same time I did.

The next day he brought in the article, ripped out of a magazine. I started reading the article but then turned to the next page to see a picture of Fritz with a nude statue. The gold statue was of a Hollywood movie star. The sculptor was Fritz, the movie star was an Italian, the gold was from Russia, and the picture was taken in Cuba. After that, I never heard anything from my friend Fritz.

College in Germany

In Germany, because of the war, the time to get a diploma was reduced by one year. The reduction eliminated the summer vacations. This was the reason for me to attend college in Germany.

It was the summer of 1941, not the best time to plan your future. World War II was raging. There were bitter confrontations on many fronts. Germany invaded Russia in June. Hungary joined the Axis and got militarily involved with the invasion of Yugoslavia and Russia.

I was protected from the draft because of my intention of pursuing higher education. To prepare to go to Germany, I had to submit my parents' and my grandparents' birth certificates to the German consulate in Budapest to prove that I wasn't Jewish. This and other paperwork completely occupied my summer. Many times I doubted that I was going to make the starting date but I made it, and left Budapest three days before college started.

The train went through Czechoslovakia, and those whose destination was Germany were moved in the front of the train because they locked the wagons. We were in Germany when the train stopped in a dark station (Germany was dark at night because of the bombing). Next to us was a freight train, apparently full of captured Russian soldiers yelling for water (I only knew it was water in 1946 when the Russians occupied Budapest). All of a sudden, the sound of a submachine gun's repeated short bursts were coming from close by. The yelling stopped, our train started off and kept going until reaching our destination, Dresden. Taking another train, I arrived in a small college town around lunch time.

I checked into the college then with the police, and found a room and bath living quarters without any problem. Next day I picked up the food stamps. They were organized by the week. There were stamps for butter, meat, bread, and cigarette. The cigarette was three per day. If you go to a restaurant, the menu called out how much meat, fat, flour, or bread tickets you had to give to the restaurant for the meal. I had to give a majority of my food tickets to the kitchen where I received three meals a day.

The whole three years were boring hard work, very little social life. The majority of the students were foreigners, lots of German girls, no German boys.

The small town was peaceful. The only signs of war were wounded German soldiers from a local hospital, French Officers from a local prisoner-of-war complex, and Russian soldiers coming and going from labor camp to work, thirty-forty in a bunch with German guards. The Russians wore wooden shoes, marching with quite a racket. The French officers kept their uniforms, some days walking and shopping around the city without any supervisors. The only restriction was that they had to walk on the road, not on the sidewalk.

According to local rumor, the hospital had a giant magnet to remove ammunition fragments from the wounded body. There was a waiting time for each patient because there were too many injured.

During the three years I was in Germany, the only sign of the war came from the radio, and was going worse and worse for the Germans. Also, the restriction and availability of food had signs of deteriorating situation. After graduation, I left the next day quite happy to reach the Hungarian border. The border agents took my passport with the remark that I can be picked up in Budapest.

* * *

I had a friend in college who was Romanian. His father was working in the Romanian embassy in Berlin. The first year at Christmas they invited me to their house located on the outskirts of Berlin. I spent three days with them, most of the time in the basement because of the bombing.

In the beginning of summer of the second year, my friend arrived with a sexually transmitted disease he said he got in Berlin. He was cured by the college doctor. To his surprise, he was called in by the local police asking him lots of questions, including the identity of his partner in Berlin who infected him. He told them a prostitute he met at one occasion, etc. Two or three weeks later they asked him back, showing twenty to thirty pictures of prostitutes working in the area where he met his prostitute. He selected one look-alike, but the police told him that was a local woman working for the police. He thought that that was it.

He was told that the next weekend he was to go to Berlin in the company of a local policeman. At that point, he admitted he was infected in Romania. Three days later, he was told to leave Germany in forty-eight hours. That was the end of the romance.

* * *

During the last year of college in Germany, I got involved with a French prisoner of war from a prisoner-of-war camp for French officers outside of the city. Every week the prisoners were allowed to go to the city for the day. They were dressed in their uniforms, only the rank was removed. They went shopping and were allowed to go into the stores.

I was shopping one afternoon with my girlfriend when I noticed a French guy was always around us, either before or behind us and writing in a notebook. When I said goodbye to my girlfriend I noticed that the French guy very carefully pointed to me to follow him. We walked next to a park with rose bushes next to the road. He took a piece of paper and hid it in the bush. I passed the bush, turned around, then took the paper out of the bush. The French guy nodded his head up and down satisfyingly. It was an envelope with a note attached to it. He asked me in German to mail the envelope. He will drop off one every two weeks in the same bush. The envelope was addressed to a German-named woman close to the French border.

I did this every two weeks up until Christmas when I found a big jar of caviar at the place of the envelope buried in the snow-covered bush with a note thanking me for the help and that he was not going to send any more envelopes. The jar was quite heavy. I took it back to the apartment and tasted it with my Hungarian friend. We ate it every night with some fresh vegetable like carrots. We did this for probably two to three weeks. After that I was unable to eat caviar for many years.

My First Job

I hardly unpacked my luggage from Germany when I got a call for an interview. My father's friend got me the interview with the vice president of engineering of one of Hungary's largest steel fabricators.

The interview was very short. The VP introduced me to his engineering manager of the research laboratory. He took me over to his office where he told what my job was going to be and asked me if I was interested. I said yes. He told me my salary and took me over to the personnel department. I started to work the next day.

I rose up early the next day because the place was an hour of city bus ride from home. The whole lab was five guys and five women, all engineers. The place was immaculate. I got my first assignment.

All day there was lots of traffic in the lab. Mostly, department managers visiting my boss and lab personnel. It was the social center of the surrounding buildings.

There was one engineer in the office and a number of visitors who were wearing a yellow Star of David (made of fabric about four inches large) fastened to the work clothes. They had it also on their jackets. The position of the star had to be specified because it had to be in the same place.

A couple of months before my arrival, the democratic Hungarian government was taken over by a Nazi-oriented group who jailed a number of high-ranking politicians from the previous administration. The new government reinforced our relationship to Hitler, established a Nazi dictatorship, and established strict rules to restrict Jewish freedom.

One of the engineers was also wearing the yellow star. He was living in a Jewish labor camp close by. He was very bitter about his situation. The Hungarians who served in the military considered the Jews serving in labor camps lucky because they were far removed from the front line and nobody was shooting at them. The general public—I don't know about the Jews—first heard about the existence of German death camps weeks after the end of the war.

The whole company was very well organized. They had generous vacation time. A big clubhouse on the shores of the Danube River, rowing club, tennis courts, etc. It was available for both the factory and office workers.

All my colleagues were friendly. After a week, I felt that I knew everybody for a long time. I met the owner the first day I was there. He was also Jewish, an industrial aristocrat. I didn't know if he got his title from the government or inherited it from his father.

He was very interested about life in Germany and my relationship to Germans in college. He was also interested in life in Switzerland and generally my experience with the Jews in Germany. I sure didn't have much to say because I heard in the college town there was an old Jewish couple but nobody knew anything about them. He visited the lab two to three times a week and most of the time he spoke to me. I did not understand his interest in me, but with my experience today I would consider him gay.

He was a good looking guy in his fifties, six feet tall with an athletic appearance, meticulously dressed, and with a happy-go-lucky personality. I didn't pay too much interest in him. My interest was on a lady engineer and the practically daily air raids.

The lady was engaged, she returned my interest with the coolest response.

Air raids were scary. The Americans were coming in early afternoons from Italy in large formation of two to three hundred planes. The Russians came in 10–11 p.m. Twenty to thirty planes with baby bombs compared to the Americans.

Very close to the lab, there was a general command bunker located underground, with four to five feet of concrete walls and ten-foot ceiling. It was a round room more than one hundred feet in diameter with a large steel door. The door and room were connected with a fifteen feet wide and thirty-foot long walk. The periphery of the round room had tables facing the wall, about twenty of them. Each table was separated from the other with a ten-inch thick concrete wall.

Each table had an attendant who had telephone connection to an observer some place in the plant. The observers mostly were on rooftops. I was one of the telephone operators. In the center of the room was a large, round table where telephone operators were connected to the outside world and bunkers throughout the whole industrial complex.

We entered the bunker when sirens outside warned of an oncoming raid. We had never been around at night, so we only faced American raids.

The Americans only targeted large industrial units. Ours was a relatively small complex located far from the big units, so the observers only told us where the bombers were coming from and where they dropped the bombs—if they could see it; also in which direction they were leaving. We waited for the sirens and went back to work.

On a Wednesday lunch time, there was again a raid. It was a sunny day. I listened to the observer telling me that the number of planes was the same as usual. There were going from south to north, west of us. Then he said they are turning right toward us. I told him to get down from the roof. I yelled to everybody what was happening. That was followed with silence.

We sat for about ten minutes when the first bomb fell. The earth was shaking. The bombing didn't stop. All of a sudden, bombs start to fall right by us. People sitting in the hallway on a long bench with their back to the wall fell face down. When they wanted to stand up another group of bombs fell close by, this group made a loud whistling sound before they exploded, then quiet.

We waited and waited until we heard the sound of the sirens. We went up. We could hardly see as the smoke was so thick. Two building close to us were burning. Also, the electric wire insulation was burning. The lab building was intact, also the bunker. We went back to the bunker; it was dark with no electricity, no telephone. We didn't know how the three thousand people in the plant survived.

It was 2:00 p.m. We stayed around until 4:00 p.m. I had no information whether or not there was transportation in the city. I went to our bus station and by some miracle the bus was coming in fifteen minutes. At home, everything was normal. We went back next day to find the lab windows were all blown out, so everybody was helping to clean up the place. This was what we did for the rest of the week. By Monday, we were doing our work like before. Nobody got injured or lost his life. The burned buildings were warehouses. Nobody from the lab was hit at home.

During the day, the owner was on his routine visit in the lab. He asked if anybody got hurt at home. The plant received limited damage. Another week and everything was going to be repaired and back to normal.

A month later, I was drafted into the army to the Special Mountain Forces. I was just rolling around like a football and becoming used to it since I have zero control over what is happening to me.

One day the owner came around for his regular visit. As he came over to my desk, he took an envelope out of his pocket, covered up the envelope and put it between other papers on my desk. He sat on my desk as usual and said, "I am leaving tonight for Switzerland. In the envelope is the key for the safe. Tomorrow morning come earlier than my secretary, put the key into the door of the safe and leave. The safe is empty." Then he left. I never even saw him in my life. The next day I put the key into the safe door. Two days later we heard (also in the newspaper) that he went to Switzerland for eye surgery.

I came back to the factory once more after the war ended. It was the law that everybody had to return to his or her workplace to prove that she or he was not a Nazi or German sympathizer. You went before a panel of six to eight people selected from local union members, Communist Party members, and reliable German haters like Jews. The panel was mostly blue-collar workers.

I had no problem since I was working such a short time that nobody knew me. Only one Jewish member of the panel asked if I remember a former Jewish manager or was I in touch with him after WWII. I told them I remember him, but after I went into military service I never saw him again. The information about him was that he ended up as a cooperator of the German commander in a labor camp and treated the Jews worse than the Germans.

Military Service

It was just two months ago that I returned from Germany finishing my college program. My first job lasted only six weeks when I got my order to report for military service in ten days.

The political and military situation in Hungary was a hopeless disaster. Budapest was bombed during the day by the Americans and at night by the Russians. The city was full of people who were escaping from the eastern part of Hungary to avoid the advancing Russians. There were columns of German trucks, tanks, etc. moving west, day and night.

The only thing I had to buy before reporting for duty was a standard wood box about the size of a small ice chest, painted green. Inside the box was a removable shelf. The purpose of the box was to keep your personal stuff. The boot camp was located close to Budapest. It was a makeshift military camp using four empty warehouses. We were about two hundred young guys in our early twenties, all high school graduates ready to be trained to become officers after about a two-year service.

After checking in, we were assembled in one of the warehouses, lined up to take the oath followed with the first military lunch. Getting new uniforms was the next job. In another warehouse, all the clothing was in one line, piled up on the floor. As you walked by, you received one or more of each item, regardless of your size. In the next room, you tried to exchange to the right size to the ones which did not fit you. I could assemble the right size—one in everything—except the boots. I had one large and one small. I got told to go to a local shoemaker close by. He would find a good pair, and he did.

The biggest problem for all of us was that there were no socks. Instead we received individual pieces of square flannels about the size of a large handkerchief. We received with detailed demonstration how to fold around our feet without cramping up our shoes. It was a definite challenge for the next few days because during different exercises, you could not take your boots off and fix the thing. Once you got the hang of it, it was quite comfortable.

All through the days, we were involved with the practice, organization, and rules of military life. Hours and hours of marching in formation regardless of pouring rain or sun or dust storms, etc. We were walking home from one of the target shooting exercises when a bunch of civilians, mostly middle aged, walked against us on the highway. There were probably five hundred of them, men and women, all Jews, wearing a large yellow star. They were guarded by Hungarian soldiers with an officer in charge. There were Jewish labor camps throughout Hungary for military-aged men under military rules. Mostly were involved with repairing roads, repairing damages after bombing etc. But this was different: men and women, all carrying small packages and guarded by soldiers. They didn't look like criminals. We were all puzzled.

After six weeks we were divided into small and large groups, mine was only ten. We were told to get on the train and go to the famous military training facility about one hundred miles from Budapest. The military situation was so bad that anything was possible.

Arriving at our location, we were picked up by a truck which drove us to a long-existing military training facility where we were told that the next two to three days would be busy with orientation, getting familiar with the new location, new uniforms, etc. We had to wait for the others to arrive to start training in four days. The place was big. Everything was in perfect shape, scrubbed and painted and not a cigarette on the ground. Bushes and trees were cut and cared for. Everybody in perfect uniforms, it was impressive.

There were many three-story buildings, a large number of long barns, warehouses, a big lot filled with trucks, vehicles, artillery trucks, etc., all around a larger-than-a-football-field-solid-dirt grounds. The surroundings were all kinds of training facilities, from multitude of obstacle courses to target shooting fields. The whole complex was surrounded with farmland sitting in a flat valley and small wooded hills as far as you could see. There was not a single building visible.

The few of us who were apparently early arrivals were assigned to bunk beds in a large room. The beds had straw-filled sacks on them, no pillow, and no cover. We got told we would get everything when everybody arrives. The room was on the third floor. There were four rooms and a large shower all in all on the same floor. In two days everybody arrived. Our room held a hundred people in bunk beds. By the door there were two single beds.

On the first day of organized action, a sergeant woke us up early in the morning, introduced himself, and stated that he would be our boss and that he would live with us and supervise us during the full term. We had breakfast and then the whole school assembled outside. A lieutenant introduced himself as the top officer. We were briefed by different officers on our upcoming program, all the rules and schedules, and so on and so forth. Then all started out with shower, medical check-up, barber, and new uniform. This was the time we got told we were all mountain specialties (which was special forces within the infantry but in normal times, ski troops).

We finished all by 6:00 p.m., then clean-up, dinner and free time, which we could spend inside or outside. By 8:00 p.m. we had to be inside. Inside, two bunk beds faced each other. That was the time for the four people sitting on either side of the bed to discuss the day's events, write letters, fix and clean uniform and boots. We still had our green wooden boxes to keep underwear, etc., organized.

A routine day started with shower, breakfast, lining up outside for briefing, reporting of new arrivals, asking for medical time off, etc. It was a rigid process conducted by the lieutenant in charge of pacing before the troops. The next event was the daily assignment for each group (one hundred soldiers). Every day the first program was the obstacle course. This was a typical three-mile run, climb, jump, crawl, up and down the course. The course was different every day. It was arranged to have the more difficult obstacles at the end of the run.

If you failed once, you have three chances to correct it. If you failed all three, the next morning you start at 4:00 a.m. cleaning up horses and the barn. There were a number of obstacles if you didn't make it in the first time or you were too exhausted to try it again.

One of them was a simple wooden fence sitting at the end of an uphill run. The wooden fence was about twelve feet wide and more than nine feet high. The problem was that it was close to the end of the run. You had to jump from a lower point (because the fence was uphill) to catch the top of the fence to pull yourself up to pass over. It was a killer.

The other one was tree elevation—single ten inches by ten inches wood logs. Construction started out about shoulder high, with two steps up, each step the same as the first one. The problem was that early morning, the wood was slippery and you have enough trouble to try to balance yourself, adding the slipping to it was too much. There were no water hazards on any course because of the season.

The food was very good because you were always hungry. The only enjoyable meal was Sunday lunch. My specialty was volunteering to pick up bread for the whole room every second night. Two of us had to go over the kitchen with a blanket. We counted out a hundred two-pound loaves and placed it into the spread out blanket. We carried it up to the room where the sergeant gave one loaf to each person. The bread was solid like a piece of brick and had to last for two days. I managed to pick up an extra loaf most of the time that we divided between two of us. I ate my half loaf after the lights were turned off in the room. The first week passed without any problems.

The most relaxing part of the day was the last hour before bedtime, when four of us, facing two bunk beds, discussed the day, told stories of the past, or read letters from home received that day. Three of us were living close to each other in Budapest but never met before. The fourth guy was living outside of Budapest. Three of us were becoming good friends. The fourth one was sticking to his own group. My friends were Peter and Joseph, the fourth guy was Miklos. Peter and I occupied the lower beds, Joseph and Miklos, the upper ones.

One night at the end of the second week, I woke up in the middle of the night. Peter was shaking Miklos, who was sleeping above him, while screaming, "You pissed on me, you S.O.B." The whole room woke up. The sergeant ran over to discover that Miklos pissed in his bed. It ended up on Peter below him. The sergeant gave Peter the only empty bed close to him on the other side of the door. Miklos was sent over to the hospital after admitting he had a bed-wetting problem. After that incident, Miklos disappeared.

The next excitement came about when one morning the daily inspection was conducted by a new officer—on horseback. His name was Bruno. He said he was transferred to the school from the Russian front. Life became hell under his direction. We never saw him walking. He was always on horseback. His guiding principle was that any one of us was better off dying here than on the front. The smallest infraction resulted in immediate punishment: twenty, thirty, fifty, etc. push-ups. He had an unlimited variety of physical abuse. There was no classroom anymore. We had to sit on the ground. Rain or shine, each individual training assignment received an extra addition from Bruno's inventory, making the simplest things difficult.

Walking was the first item in the morning. After the obstacle course, we only had to carry a rifle or a submachine gun. It usually lasted two hours with one fifteen-minute break. Under Bruno, it was two and a half hours. No break with full load: rifle plus hand gun, full load of ammunition, gas mask. The extra was wearing the gas mask for half an hour. Also the walk, slow down, speed up, and run.

The rifle target practice was done lying down, kneeling, and standing up, many of them after ten to twenty pushups. The distance was also extended. The extra addition was to take the bullets and take apart each rifle rolled in the dirt, then cleaned and shut.

In pistol practice, colored ribbons were put on each target while the sergeant called out the colors with our backs facing the target. Then, we turn around and shoot the called out color.

The hand grenade throwing was started normally. We had to line up, ten soldiers at a time, about fifty feet (fifteen meters) apart. We pulled the pin, and throw standing up or lying on the ground. The Bruno addition was we had to be lying down on our stomach, forming a large circle, with our head facing the center of the circle wearing steel helmets. The sergeant would place one hand grenade in the center of the circle then run back and wait for the grenade to explode. It was done five to ten times in a row. After it was finished you were covered with dirt, ears ringing.

All of the trails carried bad performance equals bad assignment. The extra Bruno was the horses were part of the daily morning inspection. The appearance of the horses had its own set of rules that were carved in stone.

Local rumor was that the German commander on the Russian front requested the transfer of Bruno from the front because of his brutal handling of Russian war prisoners. The transfer was approved by the Hungarian command and this is how we ended enjoying his undivided attention.

The only way we were aware of the progress of the war on many fronts in Europe and specifically in Hungary was by calling home in our free time. We had no radio to listen to. There were many air raids. It wasn't every day but it was always during the day triggered by American bombers going and coming from Budapest. The bombers, hundreds of them, fly in tight formation protected by fighters. Close to us was a military airport, lately only for Hungarian fighters. We knew that a raid was coming because all the planes there took off and returned after the Americans left. The only reason they left was to protect the planes. When our siren sounded we ran to a deeply wooded hill close by for cover.

It was early September when one morning, during the inspection, Miklos was lined up with discharge papers to report to Bruno he was going back to civilian life. He was apparently under medical observation because Bruno never learned about him. Bruno asked about his paper, read it, and ripped it up.

"You stay. Get back to your unit. I am going to cure you in no time," said Bruno. Miklos was with us all day, had dinner and went to the empty bed next to the sergeant's. The lights were turned off. I was close to falling asleep when the door opened up. A strange voice said, "Get up, we go to piss."

"I don't have to," said Miklos.

"Go," the voice said. And off they went. We found out the next day that all night every half an hour somebody took out Miklos whether he wanted or not. This went on for three nights. Then Miklos disappeared. He admitted he was faking the sickness to escape the service. He was jailed.

It was common that Bruno inspected the order of the room during the night. This was the only time he wasn't on horseback. The uniform had to be folded and placed on the top of the green wooden box. The boots next to each other, with socks folded onto them. All other items were in the wooden box. He inspected the room in the dark with a flashlight. Most of the time, the sergeant told us in the morning that Bruno was there. One night we woke up, "Out of bed," Bruno was screaming. "I have never seen a worse garbage dump than this room."

"Get in crawling position and crawl under the beds around the room. If I whistle you stand up wherever you are," he said.

He whistled three or four times and the whole room looked like it went through a hurricane. "I'm going to leave for ten minutes, and when I come back I want perfect order. If not, we can do this all night," he said. He came back and the room was in order.

We were practicing the use of revolver, rifle, submachine gun, and hand grenade. The bazooka was next. We were told this was the goal of the school, that we become experts with this weapon. In the next week, we will learn and practice all about it. There was a financial factor added to the successful use of the bazooka. The single target of the bazooka was enemy tanks. For each tank we destroyed, we would receive a five-acre land after the end of the war.

The bazooka was a shoulder-operated, five-foot tube with rocket ammunition. If it was successfully launched, the rocket hits the vertical side of the tank, sticks to it, blows a hole through the steel, and explodes. The problem was that the accuracy of the bazooka was only reliable at a short distance. The frontal visibility of the tank was very good. The side visibility was only effective with the top hatch open. The top machine gun was unable to shoot targets close to the tank. All these facts were explained and demonstrated in the next days of education, in which all arrived at the conclusion that the best way to use the bazooka was to shoot from a foxhole.

The foxhole was a round hole in the ground able to hold one person, to stand up in shooting position with arms above ground level. To dig a foxhole was challenging work because of the depth and small diameter. The area we practiced the digging was sandy dirt that made it easy to dig. But after you dig two holes in the morning, your arms were finished. The other challenge was to dig a hole under you when you were standing in the hole, since there was a limit to reach down from standing next to the hole. In total, we dug four holes each of us in two days or a total of four hundred holes covering a large area.

The third day, Bruno selected three guys who had to dig a hole. By the time they were finished, there was a tank with running engine close by. Bruno delivered a big speech about the security of the soldier camouflaged with bushes hiding in the hole. According to Bruno, the only thing tanks can do is go over the foxhole and go back and forth to bury the soldier. The tank was there to demonstrate that the tank is able to do that because of the small diameter of the hole. The soldier can stay in the hole unharmed and destroy the tank after it left.

Everything sounded logical. My opinion was that I will never intend to end up in a foxhole for three main reasons:

1. I can miss the tank or the thing does not explode.

2. Any unharmed tank can come close to the hole; one person climbs out of the tank and shoots the guy in the hole with his pistol.

3. I am a city boy; I have no use for five acres.

But since Bruno was on a different wavelength, he asked for a volunteer to go into the hole and two other guys to help out the guy from the hole. The tank came, went back and forth, turned around and left. The two helpers stood by after the tank left, waiting. Bruno was yelling to dig out the guy with their hands. They couldn't find the hole. Bruno yelled at everybody to find the hole and rescue the guy. We found the hole and dug out the guy. An ambulance came to pick him up. He recovered.

The same night during dinner, ninth of October, Bruno came into the mess hall and announced that the school was transferred to Germany. He did not know the exact day. He has scheduled visitation for relatives on Sunday, fifteenth of October. This was a shocker. Our thinking all the time was that when we were finished with school, we would be sent to the front in Hungary. It is true that in the summer of 1944 Germany occupied Hungary, but nobody suspected that we were going to be shipped to Germany to protect them from the Russians during the last days of the war.

When we went back to the room sitting around on our bunks, we had a hard time explaining our feelings. I told Peter and Joseph that one thing was for sure, I was not going to be shipped to Germany.

"So what are you going to do?" asked Peter.

"I am going to take off as soon as possible. The Russians are not far from reaching Budapest. I have to be back before they take over the city," I said.

"Are you aware that if anybody catches you between here and Budapest, or further in Budapest before the Russians take over, they can shoot you on sight?" asked Peter.

"If I get to any destination in Germany in one piece we could be ordered to fight the Russians or go into a Russian prison camp," I said. "To go home I know the route in detail, I can hide by friendly farmers and talk to anybody in Hungarian. Besides I am going to be armed, I can protect myself."

Peter said, "I am with you."

Joseph wasn't sure but finally agreed to join us.

First order of business was to telephone home. Tell the situation (without our decision to escape) and ask to bring a warm sweater, light coat, and first aid supplies on visiting day. We still had our green box with the summer clothing and shoes from the time we were enlisted. The day was tenth of October. We decided to leave the school on twenty-second of October. This was the next Sunday after the visit of relatives. This gave us close to two weeks preparation. Also visiting Sunday afternoon was when we could really move around the school because the supervising officers and staff had to return by 10 p.m.

During the remaining period, we had to get hold of two grenades, one handgun, and ammunition for each of us. The most desirable protection would be provided by a submachine gun, but to steal one was impossible. Hand grenades were the easiest to get hold of because every now and then two of them were given to each guy. Ten to twenty of us had to throw at one time. And if you were throwing from a trench far away from the sergeant, you could easily mimic the throwing (since everybody had to throw it at the same time) and cover the hand grenade with the dirt and pick it up during free time at evening and hide it some other place.

The handgun was more difficult. Before practice, it was distributed to everybody (one hundred handguns, one to each guy), also the ammunition. After practice, we had to deposit the guns into a wooden box while the magazine goes into a separate box. Also, many times, we had to keep the handgun, take it back to the room and clean it. In the remaining ten days we had three or four chances to accomplish this. The ammunition was not a problem because we practiced shooting two to three times a week and there was no problem putting five to ten bullets in your pocket.

We just had to come up with some way to pick up a handgun. We had plenty of time to do it. We never paid attention what happened to the handgun after we returned it. We didn't know if the ones returned were counted or that they have any way to keep track of it.

We kept as low a profile as possible. Do not volunteer, do not fail any assignments, be on time for any event, do not have any questions, do not ask for any favors, etc.

During free time, the three of us were never together for any reason. When visitation came, we did not introduce each other to our parents or relatives.

If during the escape we were faced with possible capture, we defend ourselves jointly and never abandon any one of us. The final solution against capture is suicide.

If any of our fellow soldiers initiate any discussion about a potential escape, we break up the discussion.

If any one of us changes his mind to proceed, we do not want to hear about it, instead the person should stay away from the starting assembly.

Germans generally do not interfere with civilians or Hungarian military.

Patrols and roadblocks by Hungarian military were the only dangerous encounters we could face during our trip home. Patrols were mostly two soldiers, no handgun but World War I rifles; they most likely would not challenge three guys in the dark. During the day is a toss-up. Both day and night we had to be vigilant to not run into them. We were in good enough shape to outrun them. Roadblocks were certain death. The only way we could reach Budapest was if we asked a truck to pick us up. Military trucks are recognizable. Private trucks would not stop seeing an upcoming roadblock. We have to be alert and jump off in time. We were aware of the consequences we were facing. To trust in our ability and physical training for the past three months was our only chance of survival.

The whole complex didn't have a fence around it. Most buildings were lit at four corners with a single light. Bushes surrounded most buildings. On one side of the camp was a field with standing corn. On one place the cornfield was about fifty feet from a building. We would hide our clothing and arms in the bushes which were close to the cornfield. Our meeting point on the night of the escape would be in the cornfield.

We discussed the details between Peter and me and whatever we agreed, Peter told Joseph.

We were successful in securing the hand grenades and bullets a week before the visit. The visit included three hundred parents of soldiers. So were the relatives of the other four hundred soldiers. We had nothing to do with the three hundred. They were specialized in the field of medical support, artillery, and transportation. We had our morning inspection together with them. Peter and Joseph had their parents visiting them while my brother and old friend from high school visiting me. The visit started at lunch time and finished by 6:00 p.m., but most left earlier to catch the train going home. We received the item we were asking for.

During our last week, we followed in very detail our agreement and we were physically and mentally prepared to escape the following Sunday.

Months after our escape (hiding in Budapest, the Russian occupation, etc.), I met with Peter a number of times but neither one of us had seen Joseph. In the late summer of 1945, I ran into George in Budapest. He was the only one who was alive returning from Germany to Budapest. He had a long story to tell about what happened after they discovered that we escaped.

According to George:

Our sergeant in charge discovered that we were missing at bedtime. He asked if anybody knew where we were but nobody knew. He told everybody to go and look for us in the shower, john, storage room, etc., but there was no trace of us. He called Bruno who came over in no time with the school's top commander. The whole floor was ordered to look for us in the building and outside. It was close to 11:00 p.m. when the search ended. Everybody returned to their room.

Our room, George said, had to line up in the hallway. Bruno was screaming at the top of his voice that if anyone was caught helping us, he himself would blow their heads off. Further, he expressed that all the ninety-seven remaining of us were involved to help us escape. Everybody knew that all three of us lived in Budapest. Also somebody knew that I had just come home from Germany. But nobody knew what I was doing there.

None of that satisfied Bruno. Screaming, he ordered us to go back to our room.

"You are going to be dressed in African combat uniform. You undress and get naked, put on your boots, belt, and helmet holding the rifle and line up here in five minutes," he said.

According to George, he never saw anything more ridiculous in his life than a group of naked guys with boots, belt, and steel helmet lined up in a cold, hardly lit hallway, shivering and waiting for what was going to happen next.

"You line up four in a row, one row behind the other, go down to crawling position, with two hands holding the rifle, and crawling on your elbows go down on the stairs," screamed Bruno. "If somebody bumped the rifle on the floor, making a noise, everybody stands up, goes back to the start, and proceeds down," he said.

"You will do this 'til somebody tells me the story of the escape." He was screaming all the time. According to George, after going and starting again, Bruno gave up and told them to go back to sleep.

After that, everything went back to normal. George was not sure when they started preparation to leave, but they had to leave the wooden boxes at the school. The day before departure, a long wagon train arrived loaded up with food, ammunition, benches, tables, etc. Also, all four hundred soldiers, staff, and four officers, including Bruno established a temporary home in the wagon.

According to George, the trip took ten days. Many times the train waiting for hours on stations some place in Germany. Finally they arrived at an empty German military camp located south of Berlin close to the Polish border. It took more than a week to get organized. In the meantime, the school's top brass and the officers' family arrived. It was early January.

Apparently, the top officers of the school were in contact with the German military because there were daily meetings with everybody present about the progress of the Russians. One late afternoon, German officers took part in the briefing. They expected the Russian army to reach the camp. The Germans approved that the school's top officer make the decision how to proceed.

Next morning, they were told that Bruno killed his wife and children. George said this was enough for him to take off. He walked half day to reach a small German town. The town was empty—not a living person in sight. He was looking for food but could find only one carrot still in the ground. He was hiding in an empty closet when the Russians arrived to the town.

He went back to the camp hoping to find civilian clothing while passing Russian soldiers. They did not pay attention to him. Walking next to a railroad track, he ran into our sergeant. He told George not to go back. The only thing he would find would be frozen bodies. After Bruno killed his family, the sergeant said everybody agreed to oppose the Russians. As the Russians closed in, Bruno and a dozen soldiers started to machine gun the Russians.

They stopped and moved back. They started their artillery and later tanks, and killed everybody. The sergeant took off when Bruno started shouting then hid under a small bridge until the first column of Russians passed him. George said he joined the sergeant all the way back to the Austrian-Hungarian border where they split up— the sergeant going south and George back home to Budapest.

Escape

It was pitch dark and cold when I arrived at our meeting place. I was the first one. The standing corn gave perfect cover but was unnecessary because of the dark. Peter and Joseph arrived shortly after me. We picked up our ammunition and clothing and moved further into the cornfield. We had to move slowly and not make any noise.

As we were walking, we discovered that there was a road in the distance with car traffic. After changing into civilian clothing (partially originating from the wood box but mainly from our visiting relatives), we carefully walked closer and closer to the highway which was visible by the lights of the cars.

During the walk, we discovered that the two hand grenades were very bulky and therefore possibly suspicious, so each of us kept only one and dropped the other ones. We all had handguns with plenty of bullets.

The highway ran east to west, which was perfect for us. Budapest was southeast from us. The cornfield was on both sides of the highway, so we went close enough while avoiding the bright light of the cars. We were walking for an hour when we discovered that a good distance from us was an intersection. Getting closer, we saw people waiting and hoping for a ride.

It should be noted here that Hungary was in a panic trying to move to the west before the Russians. We realized that all the people in the intersection intended to go west. Probably we were the only one to go east. We joined the group and didn't have to wait long when a medium-sized truck with canvas stopped. Peter ran to the driver and told him where we intended to go. The driver motioned us to climb up.

In the truck were half a dozen people. We settled down so that we could watch through the driver's back window the road before us. We were going more than two hours when Peter jumped up and motioned to the driver that we wanted to get out. Not even waiting for the truck to stop, we jumped off and ran into the woods on the south side of the road. There was a roadblock about a mile ahead. The whole location was lit up by standing cars and people with flashlights standing and walking. We could not see whether it was a German or Hungarian roadblock but we were just happy that Peter saw it from a distance.

The problem was that the woods stood at the edge of a large empty field. Walking away from the highway, the woods gave us cover for about two hundred yards or two football fields. In the meantime, the moon came out. We had to walk back to the west then a good distance from the highway. By the time we were back to the road, it was two hours after midnight, and we were not even halfway home. Walking a good distance parallel to the highway, on plowed farmland, was very difficult. Our guess was that we were about a one-hour drive from the road going north.

The traffic became minimal, none going east. We were talking about that if we could find the right cover we would take a nap and hunker down for the day, when a truck came from the west. It was loaded with hay. We motioned for him to stop. There was a woman sitting next to the driver. I told him that we intended to go north—to Budapest. He said he was going further east than the northbound highway but he could stop by the intersection. I asked him not to stop by the intersection but go further east because one of us lived close by. He said we were about an hour's drive from the road going north. There was no room in the back of the truck but we could squeeze ourselves between the cab and hay.

Passing the intersection, we got off. After the truck left, we discovered that in a distance, two soldiers with rifles on their shoulders were walking east. They stopped for the passing truck and looked in our direction but didn't pay attention and kept walking. We very slowly started walking in the opposite direction. We had to avoid walking north on the highway as we were concerned about military traffic.

The intersection was sitting in the middle of a town surrounded by private homes. It was still dark when we started walking north parallel to the highway. After we reached the end of the town, we went close to the highway and continued walking some distance in a grassy field. German flatbed military trucks were the only traffic going north, but they were going too fast to jump in the back. After walking about half an hour, we reached a small hill. A German truck going north slowed down halfway up on the hill to change gears. The location was perfect for us.

On both sides of the road there were large trees close to the road with large bushes between the trees. We were close to the location when another German truck came from a distance away and slowed down, giving us the perfect chance to jump on the back. We also noticed they were carrying wooden boxes covered with black tarp. We covered ourselves with the black tarp. It was early morning when we recognized where we were and jumped off rolling into the ditch next to the road.

I was about half an hour away from my home. Peter and Joseph lived in different directions. We got rid of the hand grenades and said goodbye, knowing that we were never going to see each other again.

Hiding

As I was walking home, I realized that the most dangerous part of my effort to survive was over, but the "shot on sight" reality was in effect until the war was over or more practically, until my location was taken over by the Russians.

My home was a condo, located on the first floor of a five-story building. I was born in this condo as was my younger brother. Everybody knew me not just in the condo but in the neighborhood, and everybody knew I was drafted four months ago. Staying home or hiding at home would endanger my father and my brother, my aunt and our housekeeper who was living with us. My father was highly respected by everybody but it was too big of a gamble to try to hide at home. The other danger was the practically daily bombing of the city. In case of a direct hit of the condo, the bomb shelter provided the only escape for survival. It was located in the basement. The bombing lasted two to four hours, and the large shelter held not only the people from the condo but also—because the bombing was during the day— people from the street.

My arrival was disturbing everybody at home. My father was crying and asked me to leave. But after everybody settled down, I got a big breakfast, a shower, and clean clothing, and then we searched for some place to hide. The logical choice was my father's friend who lived in a large condo. My father and his friend agreed that early in the evening he would come and pick me up. He was in the military reserve as a lieutenant.

He came in uniform. He told me to bring the minimal stuff with me because my brother could bring things over after I was established.

Early in the evening, we used the city car to go over to the west side of the city to his condo. To my big surprise, when we arrived, we were met by the condo's manager who told me he had a hiding place in the basement next to the elevator landing. The room was a machine shop for the elevator. He pulled a large cabinet away from the wall and behind it was a door-sized opening and a small room and a short guy in his forties. After the manager moved the cabinet back, the guy named Robi explained to me that his girlfriend lived in one of the condos in the building, and that he was Jewish, and had been hiding there for the past month after having escaped from a labor camp.

The room was well lit, had a kitchen sink and a toilet in one corner behind a small brick wall. The place had two cots, a shelf with books, and food. He explained the daily routine that included a visit by his girlfriend and bringing fresh food for lunch.

We didn't have any communication with the outside world. He didn't know what was going to change with my presence.

It was late October and I was locked with a stranger, hoping that the war passes over us and we could return to some kind of life in a free Hungary to start from square one. I was expecting a real rough start with basic survival going to be the only problem. The war was grinding closer and closer. Our daily guest was Rose, Robi's girlfriend, who kept us up to date on the advances of the Russians and the life around the neighborhood. The fight for the city was already in full force.

The Danube River, flowing from north to south, divided the city. The west side is Buda, the east side is Pest. Buda is hilly, Pest is flat. The two sides are connected by eight bridges. The Danube River is about three hundred yards wide and it is a shipping route from the center of Europe to the east. The city was home to a million people, the larger part living in Pest. The Russians were coming from the east.

They crossed the river from the south and encircled the city by the end of December.

My father's friend's home was in Pest, which is about a mile from the river on one of the major roads going east. It was in the center of the city. By near Christmas for close to two months we lived in partial seclusion. Partial because we were spending more and more time with our hosts as the bombing was slowing down because of the advancement of the Russian troops. The buildings on the Pest side were all five- to six-story apartments, and the German and Hungarian troops were located on the ground levels of the buildings.

The last month of fighting was house to house. We could peek out from the large steel gate of the building. The street was empty. There were few burned out cars and dead bodies on the road, both military and civilian. The wide sidewalks were full of broken glass. It was spooky. There was no electricity after Christmas. It was freezing cold. In the apartment, most windows were broken; the only thing that was working was the water. Our basement was comfortably warm.

My host had a large supply of food including: two big sacks of melba toast, butter, lard, egg, milk powder, a variety of smoked meat, coffee, etc. He had friends all over the city and kept in touch with them daily. I lost telephone connection with my father in early December. By January, we hardly used our basement hideout. It was only there as a last resort. There were no German or Hungarian soldiers in sight.

The bottom two floors and a large part of the basement were occupied by a department store. If the sound of mortar fire was coming closer, we ended up in the bomb shelter. I slowly met most of the occupants of the condo in the shelter. It was a mixed group of young and old and Christians and Jews.

Most discussion involved planning of what the occupation of the city would do to our immediate future. How long it was going to be until life returned to "normal." In the meantime, the neighborhood discovered access to the department store, and people came in groups to help themselves to free shopping. People were using candles to search for clothing, liquor, and food to steal, and carried everything home regardless of the continuous incoming mortar fire. I was looking for food when in one corner I discovered two, dead drunk German soldiers drinking and pouring wine on the floor next to them. Nobody bothered with them. The people from the condo organized twenty-four hour house watch to protect the building from fire. People were walking in knee-high discarded paper wrapping.

One morning in early January, while all of us were staying in the bomb shelter (because of the closeness of mortars and machine guns), three Russian soldiers entered the shelter. Everybody had their hands up, some clapping. The Russians walked around. If somebody let his hand down they motion to keep up. They inspected the whole room then went from one man to another to steal their wristwatches.

Nobody spoke Russian in the group, but we understood they were looking for Germans as they held their submachine gun in ready position. We waited for them to leave and went out to the street. There were lots of Russians on foot, in trucks, all over. There was a group of people who were butchering the frozen carcass of a horse. The place was a disaster.

Russian Occupation

The occupation started with a dark to morning curfew. The Russian occupation forces were different from the initial wave of fighting troops. This group was small in number, well-equipped and aggressive. The occupiers were thieves.

Thank god for the cold weather. The streets were cleared of dead bodies in the first days of the occupation, but the store fronts were full of corpses stacked on top of each other. The only traffic on the streets was Russian military vehicles. Civilians were picked up by Russians and deported to Russian labor camps.

On the second day of the occupation, I started out from our condo to go across the river to find out what was going on with my father and brother. The Danube was a short walk. When I got to the river, I discovered that two bridges visible from my position were blown up. The steel structure of one of them was under water. The other was only ruined on the Buda side. The upper structure was standing, only the road of the bridge was partially submerged.

Looking over the other side of the river, I only could see limited damage to the buildings. There were two hills close to the river. The one right across from me had a steep slope facing the river. The other one was occupied on the south side by a royal castle, a large building complex originating from the thirteenth century. It was Hungary's most treasured jewel— a prime tourist attraction housing an irreplaceable collection of paintings, furniture, carpet, drapery, etc.

Smoke was coming out from most of the windows. It was left untouched by the Germans and burned down by the Russians. The name of the hill was Castle Hill. The north side of the hill was a collection of eighteenth century buildings, famous churches, priceless museums, etc.

Looking north from my position on my side of the river Budapest's most luxurious hotel line was burned to the ground. I had a feeling that the best I could do for my future was to get the hell out of Hungary because this place would not be able to be rebuilt in my lifetime.

Further north was a pontoon bridge built by the Russians for military traffic. There was no way I could get to the other side in the near future since all of the other bridges were destroyed. My only hope was that the telephone lines would be back faster than any repair of the bridges.

Going home, I saw a group of German prisoners of war guarded by Russian soldiers walking west. They were close to two hundred. Some of them, wounded, walked with bandages on their head, arms, etc. It was a sorry looking bunch with dirty uniforms—misery written on their faces.

Also there was a Russian truck with lots of people lined up behind it. Getting closer, two Russian soldiers were giving the people flour, measuring it out with a steel helmet. One soldier, full of flour, was collecting the rings and proofing it by biting it. I was tired and disgusted upon arriving home.

I looked at the whole situation from my perspective. I was twenty-three years old and survived WWII and also one of four from one hundred who survived the military services, healthy, have a profession, and practical enough to make the best of any given situation. The problem was that it would take a couple of years to try to create a future in a country that is on its knees. There was nothing available that was reliable to support its minimum existence. There was no health care, personal security, and safety.

There was no food, no hygiene (we had to wear the same clothes for weeks), no heating, no money, no job, etc. All of these was not just for me but also for everybody around me. We were a losing country under military occupation. There was no electricity, no telephone, no transportation, no government, and no police. There was no authority to organize anything. You can have a minor infection and be dead in no time. I had no way of knowing whether my father and brother are even alive.

The Russian occupiers were a strange group of people. Only few Hungarians spoke Russian. There was no reason for communication.

The Russian officers were well-dressed, unfriendly, suspicious, and travelled in groups of two or more. The soldiers were carrying submachine guns. They were primitive and never saw a toilet or bathtub.

They did not smoke cigarettes but made their own: having in one pocket a newspaper and in another, dried tobacco leaves. First they made a funnel from the newspaper then filled it up with hand-crumpled tobacco. Then they lit a large match by striking it on their pants, light the top of the funnel and after creating a foot-tall flame, start smoking.

Their major occupation was collecting valuables. Big choice were wristwatches. Some of them had a dozen of them as a trophy that they hung on their neck. They went from apartment to apartment, stealing clothing, shoes, gloves, etc.—whatever they considered valuable. They cut out the canvas from the frame of paintings to keep their jeeps warm when parked. After dark, they raped any female from twelve to fifteen or older while five to six of them were standing in line.

It was a major problem for every family to find hiding places for female members. For the victims, the tragedy of the act wasn't the only problem, there was also the possibility of infection and disease. There was very limited availability of doctors' help and medication.

There were also lots of Russian women in military service. They were mostly visible directing traffic, driving trucks, cleaning equipment, etc. They were also very unfriendly. Their interactions with male soldiers were always loud and confrontational. Their clothing was bulky, dirty, and generally unorganized.

Health care was nonexistent. Hospitals had limited personnel. Private doctors faced physical problems (no windows, damaged equipment) but were limited by availability of medicine.

In our area, water was available. It was a miracle because it was close to the end of February and temperatures were freezing and most apartments without windows were freezing inside. Our apartment had no working central heating. The solution was to get a small portable steel furnace and wood or coal. Some area in our neighborhood had oak trees.

There was also a local crime problem. The Russians enforced a dark to dusk curfew. There was no power in the city. There was an invisible order of decency covering the city. Nobody could stop the Russians since there was no Hungarian organization representing the city.

Our condo organized a four person group who guarded only the entrance to the buildings. The four men held guard for four hours and three times during the night behind the closed entrance door. Behind them were a disorganized group of cabinets, tables, and chairs—forcing any potential intruder to climb over a bunch of furniture.

The four men couldn't stop the Russians from entering the building, but their presence and the mess behind them hopefully made the entry uncomfortable.

A citywide problem was that organized gangs captured mostly men during the first hours of darkness. They took all their clothing and ran away with it, leaving the victim naked in freezing weather. They were mostly men because no women would go out in the dark.

One of the four-man group told the story that early one evening, a stark naked, middle-aged drunk opened the door yelling that a person had hit him on the head at the corner of the house, undressed him, and ran away with his clothing. When two guards went out, they noticed a bunch of clothing at the base of a light post. Apparently the drunk ran into the lamppost, hit his head, and then he took his clothes off thinking he was robbed. The clothes' value was what could be bartered for food.

The other local crime was the stealing of valuables from empty apartments. This included everything from furniture to clothing, anything that wasn't nailed down. The victims were people who left their apartment to move west or joined their family members located some other place.

Food was no problem initially. There was no refrigeration in the Hungarian kitchen. During the summer and fall it was standard procedure to collect and preserve food for the winter. Fruits like peaches, pears, apricots, and cherries were prepared and kept in glass jars or processed for jam. During the fall, a pig or two were butchered per family in the backyard. The lard was stored for the whole year in large steel containers, the legs used for the ham, and the rest turned into smoked sausages and consumed during winter. Most city folks had country relatives who raised and prepared them. The rest purchased the same from local butchers.

Our immediate problem was to make one room livable and the whole apartment clean and protected from snow and rain. There were three of us in the apartment: the host, his wife, and me. The apartment was located on the second floor of the building. Three rooms faced the street. The kitchen, the bathroom, and the maid's room faced the inner courtyard. Every room's window has no glass.

We selected the smallest room on the street side and the kitchen to try to make livable because both had small windows. We nailed carpets to the window frames. All three of us slept on the floor in order to use the available two large feather beds.

We were just getting used to living in an unheated room when two more miracles happened. One was we had gas, meaning we could cook and take showers using the gas water heater in the bathroom. The second miracle was that Bill's friend found a small wood-burning furnace. Since our condo had central heating, we didn't have a chimney. The furnace came with an L-shaped chimney. We cut a big hole in one of the rugs in our "bedroom." The chimney insulator was used to insulate and fasten the chimney by the hole in the carpet. All of a sudden the whole place was livable.

In the meantime, outside, limited progress was accomplished. Sidewalks were cleaned from broken glass and fallen bricks from bombed buildings. Fallen trees disappeared fast for heating.

Electricity was restarted. Four or five flatbeds were pulled by an electric car. The flatbeds loaded two to three layers of corpses. The destination point was a large cemetery east of the city where the corpses were dumped in large, long trenches.

People were travelling in the right direction filled every place next to the corpses on and on corpses the hitches between the flatbeds. The bodies were men and women, civilians and soldiers, Hungarians and Germans, excluding Russians who were taken care of the first days after the fighting. This process was going on for weeks fortunately still in freezing weather.

The business life started out by a serving hot coffee by a famous downtown restaurant. They accepted a token amount of Hungarian currency which was in bad inflation. It was only accepted by workers who took part in the initial cleaning and repair operations of the city, including its business establishments and factories. The pay was for one day only because the next day it probably wasn't worth more than one tenth. This went on for several months until the new government started printing a new currency.

Anything that was of any value, including food, was sold for the American dollar. Swiss francs kept this value also. The English pound was worthless because the Germans printed perfect copies that only experts can recognize from the real one.

The main exchange of goods was through barter. A few weeks after the roads and sidewalks were cleaned up, people lined up on the sidewalks offering a variety of stuff, mostly practical items necessary for the current situation. The price was either a dollar or something that the buyer was offering for exchange. The most valuable items were: matches, candles, kerosene, soap, tobacco, and cigarettes.

This was the beginning. Then it expanded to food items like lard, salt, flour, oil, sugar, and then to any item that, in peacetime, was offered in grocery stores, bakery stores, and butchers. A fully processed pork meat was available for a grand piano or a goose for a winter coat or a new boot. A ten-dollar bill was sold for eleven single dollars because single dollars were mostly used for food and the server was a farmer who did not have change. For farmers, the preferred item for exchange was salt, the dollar was the second choice.

Finally, the Russians allowed foot traffic on the pontoon bridge on certain hours of the day. On the first day the bridge was opened, I went home to see my father and brother. I found them in good shape and in confused spirit. Our condo was on the first floor of the building. Two rooms faced outside while the entry, the third room, the bathroom, the kitchen, and the maid's room faced the inner court. The two rooms outside were collapsed into the basement, buried with the collapsed five stories above it.

As my brother explained to me, the whole side of the building was for two weeks the first line of defense for the Germans against the Russian troops coming from the south. The standing part of the condo was usable but too dangerous to live in because the whole remaining damaged side of the building could collapse at any minute.

My father's store was on the street side of the building. That side was in good shape and had a large storage room behind it with a wood-burning stove and sink but no bathroom. Luckily, one of my father's friends (whose wife was my godmother) living on the second flood offered my father and brother the use of their bathroom. All of this was temporary. There was a long time before my father reopened his business.

My brother was graduating from high school and was planning to attend an agricultural school that was walking distance from the condo. All of my clothes were stored in a large closet in the entry room. I picked up the necessary items and agreed with my father and brother that any one of them can come over and visit us at any given day and hour.

Walking home just like I did placed me in constant danger of being picked up by the Russians and shipped into a Russian labor camp indefinitely.

The rumor was that a small number of German military and Hungarians held Budapest for several months. After the city was captured, only a small number of war prisoners were delivered— giving the Russian generals a bad mark. This was the reason they picked up and deported anybody who was of military age.

To avoid this, you have to travel on roads where you can see far ahead and be very careful at intersections where there was no way you can avoid lurking Russian soldiers.

I have told you the story of my friend who was transferred to Germany after three of us deserted the military. He was the only one besides us who survived WWII. He took off from the German camp and returned to Budapest where I accidentally ran into him. I did not see him for weeks after the meeting. He came to our condo to visit and told me the following:

Shortly after we met, he was picked up by the Russians in Budapest. He was sent to a former military camp where he stayed for more than a week. There were more than a thousand captives there. All ages up to fifty years old. They were fed and slept on straw waiting to be shipped out.

The security was well organized and the place had concrete fence around. Guards kept watch day and night on every section of the fence. He said he was aware that they were going to be shipped to Russia by train. He decided to escape from the train during the trip because regardless of the method of escape, he had to land on Hungarian ground in order to survive possible injury.

He tried to visualize a number of possible escapes but gave up planning because everything depended on the efficiency of the Russians guarding the train. He did two things for preparation, he collected bread for survival and ripped and washed any soft cloth he could find for bandages in case of injury.

When the train arrived, he checked the hitch connection between the wagons. He discovered some connections had a steel drop hanging close to the ground. That canceled out escape from the bottom of the wagon. All the prisoners were lined up thirty per wagon (forty being the top capacity). During the line up, he picked a wagon close to the end of the train to protect himself from obstructions close to the side of the train which would push him under the train. Finally, he ended up in the fourth wagon from the back.

Once in the wagon, he discovered that each door had two locks. One lock was accessible only from the inside while the other from both sides. The Hungarian-Russian border was about one hundred miles from Budapest. The train started out early in the afternoon and it was a stop and go situation. When the train stopped at a curve he could observe where the guards were located because most of the time they got off and walked back and forth next to the wagons. He had a collection of rusty steel pieces to aid him to escape.

During the first hours of travel he concluded that there was only one way to escape—pull the lock to open position from the inside. The lower lock, the one which would open only from the outside, was the one the Russians used to close the wagon.

Late in the afternoon, the train stopped by a station. They opened the doors and took one prisoner from each wagon to carry water and food to each wagon. Everybody got off to stretch their muscles and also to do their thing in the field next to the train. This included lots of yelling and warning shots in the air if prisoners went too far from the train.

Once outside, he could check out the lock. The lock was pivoted on a single shaft from a closed to open position. It was turned from horizontal close position at 180 degrees to horizontal open position. There was a round eye in the door in which the lock cleared the eye. It was open, so if there was a rope or wire attached to the handle of the door and the end of the rope and the wire moved inside the wagon, the lock could be lifted out of the eye and the door was open. He realized that nothing can hang on the lock that was visible to the Russians. So the last resort was to see if there was an opening between the door and the frame in close positions he could push the wire to the outside. The wire had a hook on one end to pull the lock open. It was perfect.

This method of escape was possible to execute without the people in the wagon knowing in advance about it. It was understandable that everybody wanted to take part in the escape but it had the potential of trouble.

Once the train was ready to continue, the doors were closed again. He settled down to sleep next to the door opening. After dark, everybody settled down. The whole group was saying a prayer as last act of the day. He fixed the wire hook and tried it out. It was working. He kept the lock open and opened the door just a hair open. His plan was to wait until the train stopped, and once it would start again, he would jump off after the train as it picked up speed (but not too fast). It was dark when it first stopped. It waited for a long time then started off again. He stood up and jumped off at the right moment. He flew against a wooden fence, stood up, and looked at the departing train, but it was too dark to see anything. After three days, he was back in Budapest.

The whole story was in my mind as I was walking home after visiting my father. At home, everybody was happy hearing my father and brother survived the war and that they were healthy. My life improved as decent clothing and normal exchange became available. We were back to cleaning and hunting for some fresh food like eggs, butter, fruits, and vegetables. All were available for dollars. Bill had a head waiter friend who had unlimited access to anything that was not available on the general exchange market like fresh fish, meat, etc.

Bill was working for the only sheet glass factory in Hungary before WWII. The factory was Belgian-owned, and Bill and the president regularly came together to keep in touch with the factory which was located in a small town away from Budapest. Bill also knew every glass installer in the city. It did not take a long time to locate somebody who could fix a broken window in the apartment, and this represented absolute luxury for the three of us. The only thing missing was electricity.

One morning, I went to visit my aunt who was living about half an hour from us. She had a street side business of female underwear and lived behind the shop. I found her in good spirits, working already. Coming home I turned into a small street. There was a large military truck full of some things in the bags. They stopped and told me to carry the bags into a house. There were already two other guys unloading the truck. I started taking a single bag into a small warehouse. The bag weighed 110 pounds and was full of salt. Salt was gold for farmers who butchered pigs for their own consumption because salt was the only preservatives they used. When we were close to finishing the job, I told the Russians to put two bags on my back. I dropped the second bag between the two bushes on the way to the warehouse. I could drop four bags hoping that in the next days I could recover them. I was lucky because after the work was finished they let us go. The next day, I made four trips to take the salt home.

It was the end of April 1945 when we finally had electricity. The apartment returned to the peacetime appearance. I had my room and Bill and his wife slept in their own bedroom.

I was on my way to attend my first business meeting when I was picked up by three Russian soldiers asking for identification. They kept my papers and told me to jump on a truck. There were already a dozen people on the truck. Nobody knew what was going on. I jumped down and took one of my shoes and pretended to remove an imaginary stone from the shoe hoping that somehow I could take off. But one guy was watching me like a hawk, and when I was finished, he motioned me to get up. They filled the truck and drove us for a good hour to a Hungarian military complex off the beaten path. It was standing alone in nowhere. The place was the size of three to four football fields with five large three-story buildings, lots of warehouses, a tall chimney, dozens of roof-only steel shelters, a large water tower, etc.

Leaving the truck, we were directed to a table with two people sitting, one was a Russian officer the other, a civilian. The civilian asked a few questions that he translated to the Russian. In a box were all the identifications that they picked up before. The civilian stamped mine and gave it back to me. I asked how long we were going to stay there, he did not answer. Then I asked where we were going from there. "You guys are here because we are going to work on a bridge close by," he said. He told us to wait until everybody was registered and he would show us where we were going to stay. It was a large building. He took us to a long room on the ground floor. The center of the room was a walk. Two sides had straw on the floor and a dirty blanket for each person. There were showers and toilets on one end as it was a standard military installation for sleeping quarters except that it had missing bunk beds. The second building had a Red Cross mark on it on the door. The whole place looked like it went through lots of action. The Russian soldiers were working outside while people were moving furniture, boxes, chairs, etc. Trucks and cars were coming and going. We were the only civilian group sitting around the benches. During the day, more trucks arrived with Hungarians. Everybody was wondering about what was going to happen.

For me, the future was obvious. There was a single train line coming in and out from the complex with steel gates on both sides. Once they collected enough people, they were going to load them up on a train and—goodbye Hungary. I still had every detail of the escape of my friend in my memory. I considered waiting to escape from there before they loaded us up into the train. At this point, I didn't know how the place was guarded. I knew the place had one guard at the entry and also one by the exit. Two unguarded train gates. The whole complex was fenced with a concrete fence without barbed wires on the top. The height was the same as the training fence in the former military facility that we jumped over during morning runs (repeatedly).

By the evening, we were about two hundred. All ages, all backgrounds.

I was in the young group, in good shape, educated. We were all certain that we were going to end in Russian labor camps. Nobody was talking about possible escape because we were certain that if they captured us, we would be executed. The first day ended up with a piece of bread and soup. They locked the room for the evening. The windows were small and only opened and closed on the top.

My homework for the evening was to develop priorities to prepare myself for escape. I was assuming that everybody was going to be picked up and shipped out via the train as the most plausible scenario. This also meant that the camp was empty and less guarded for one or two days. The camp was less guarded during the day, so I had to check out first where the guards were when the camp was full or empty. If I find such place, I had to store some water and food because I can only come out of hiding when there are new prisoners in the camp. It was also important to know what was outside of the fence after I escaped. When we arrived it looked like the camp was sitting alone surrounded by empty fields, but I was not certain.

The next day we were split up in groups and directed by a Russian to do what looked like busy work: cleaning trucks, hauling garbage, digging ditches, etc. Doing all kinds of stuff gave me a change to be familiar of the whole place. The only place I could see guards was by the gate.

There was no way I could see anything behind the concrete fence. To locate a hiding place was a problem. There were lots of buildings that looked like they had never been used as most were empty or seldom used. It was impossible to trust them for protection day and night. I was giving up looking for one when I practically ran into a flight of stairs going underground. The stairs were covered with overgrown bushes. There was a crumbling, half-open wooden door going into a place, the inside not visible. There was too much action going on in the surrounding area to try to investigate what was inside. The place was continuously receiving more and more prisoners. My last goal for the day was to check out if there were more guards on the location at night than during the day. Since we were locked inside of our sleeping quarters, my visibility was limited. I could only see from out the window the entrance and the section of the fence including the one gate for the train. This gate had a number of guards sitting on benches.

During the night, the whole place had lights on the corner of the fences with well-lit areas by the gates. The front of most buildings was also lit. There were few lights on the top of the fences and on top of the water tower. My conclusion for the day was that regardless of what upcoming day the train would depart, I have to hide at the underground place to be more familiar with the escape route and then reappear again when the first group arrives. There were many variables in the upcoming events that I can't foresee, but I was satisfied there was a good chance to escape.

The third day was very much the same as the second: with all kinds of programs initiated by the Russians. During my spare time, I walked by the hideout. I picked up a large bush and tried to pull it out in order to look inside. To my surprise, the steps were submerged in water. A large diameter, rusty pipe was crossing the inside with large shelves on both sides of the room. The shelf was full of rusty boxes and cans. The whole place looked like it was abandoned a long time ago.

The following two days, I collected bread and water and hid in the bushes next to the steps of the hideout. Before falling asleep, I concluded that I can sleep and rest on the shelf for days waiting out the best opportunity to take off or leave the hideout and mix with the new arrivals probably two to three times before the Russians discover that I never left.

About a week later the train arrived. It was early in the morning. We just finished breakfast consisting of a piece of bread and three carrots. After getting out of the building, I picked a piece of lumber, took it to the hideout and pushed it inside like I was ordered to do it and disappeared inside. At least, thinking how clever I was gave me a peace of mind. There was lots of yelling going on while the train was loaded up. Then I could hear as they closed the doors. I was expecting the train to leave soon, but it remained there until it got dark. Again there was lots of yelling as they closed the two big gates. Then it fell quiet. I looked out and it was pitch-dark. The fence was about a football field length away from me. In a distance there was a single light on the top of the fence and further down another light at the corner of the fence. From my hideout, I couldn't see the entry gate. I decided to wait until 2:00 a.m. for my escape (assuming everybody will fall into sleep deep; even the night guards lost their awareness). Also, I decided that after I was on the other side of the fence, I would sleep at the nearest cover and stay there until I can locate the safest way to leave the place.

I couldn't wait until two o'clock. Instead I started crawling for the fence close to 1:00 a.m. When I reached close enough, I jumped up, ran, and swung over the fence. There was a small ditch next to the fence on the other side. As far as I can see, there were grassy fields. By the corner of the complex there was a ditch going in the direction of a town with a few lamps. I had to cover a good distance to reach the ditch from the corner of the fence which was lit up. I had to crawl until I reached the ditch. I was finally able to stand up at the ditch which had thick bushes on both sides. Getting closer to the town, it was eight to ten houses with a road in the center. I was afraid to wake up anybody because there was a possibility that the Russian officers, the bosses of the military complex, occupied it. I went to the next town. The first store was a butcher. They let me in to clean up, gave me a clean shirt, and a windbreaker. The same day I was home, and a week later I got married.

Smuggling

One of Bill's friends, Laci, was a stock broker. During WWI, he spent four years in Russia as a prisoner of war. He came home with a Russian wife. Starting on the first part of June, he visited often and this is how I met him. There was no stock market, instead there was an open market around the stock market building buying and selling foreign currency (mostly dollar), silver and gold coins and silver and gold jewelries. Bill rented a small store across the stock market building. I joined Bill and started buying and selling gold coins, mostly French Napoleons. It was the size of a penny but much thinner. The exchange was in dollars. One Napoleon was worth eleven to thirteen dollars depending on the daily sentiment of the "market." A new ten-dollar bill was worth eleven dollars and a dirty, one-dollar bill was only worth ninety cents. A new shiny Napoleon was worth more than a scratched-up one.

Then there was the art of making twenty-one-dollar bill to twenty-one one-dollar bill. This was a precise process done by slicing and edge-gluing slices of dollar bills by making twenty bills each shorter until you end up with a free one dollar bill.

Laci's visits with his wife became more and more frequent. They sat down on one corner of the living room and talked to each other very quietly. If asked what the secret was, they would talk about the old times. My suspicion was that they were doing some business that was through Laci's connection to the Russian military. As I mentioned before, Laci's wife was Russian and both spoke fluent

Russian. Also both were working for the Russians. She was a translator and he was an advisor. They exchanged packages that I helped carry to Bill's office at the stock market. This happened two or three times before they asked me to sit down with them. Laci said that high ranking Russian officers try to cash in their gold that originated from captured Germans. Cash was dollars that they can take back to Russia. They asked me to carry packages including dollars and gold. I had to keep this a secret and Laci will pay me for each transaction.

Between my own Napoleon business and the new carrier job, I was making three hundred to five hundred dollars a month. This was three to four months after the occupation. This was also in a time when a four-person family could survive on ten dollars a month. This was only for food because there were no other expenses. There was no rent, no gas, no electricity, no mail, no transportation, no anything.

We worked our way into September of 1945 when Laci came to visit with a big smile. He discovered a new business opportunity. He said he met a Russian officer who had a pool of trucks and cars that he could provide with drivers. He also had the papers for the passengers and the cargo. He had no idea what the Russians will ask, what the limit was, when they could go, who pays for the driver's room and board, etc. We made a list for Laci to check out. We also agreed that Laci was going to be the one who dealt with the Russians.

For days we, Bill and I, went over many details to try to figure out what we could do, the limit we could spend and mainly, what we intended to buy. We have no problem what to sell or exchange. The most profitable market would be Austria (per agreement) because industrial products were cheaper there and food was in short supply. We know this from Hungarians who recently returned from there. Vienna was one hundred twenty miles from Budapest. It was damaged a lot less than Hungary. The city was divided in four zones: USA, English, French, and Russian. The military occupation of each zone was effective. Pedestrians can freely go from one to the other, but restricted for cars and trucks.

Laci returned with answers after a couple of days. The price of a three-day trip was one hundred dollars—including the driver and a three-ton truck. There is room for two people and no more. The truck can't be used for transporting people. We agreed with Laci that we need some time to do our homework. The biggest problem was who was going to be my partner for the trip. The problem wasn't that we couldn't find a person who was available for a three- to four-day trip for good pay. The problem was that the trip represented personal security risks—risks that I also faced. We concluded that we would pay all the expenses plus 15% of the profit. We spread this offer between friends. We had a few people interested. After interviewing three of them, we selected Miklos, who spoke some Russian and good German. He was a teacher, about ten years older than me, married, and happy to make some money. He and his wife lived close by in a small apartment and he supported his wife and himself by doing work in the neighborhood.

With Bill we made the following decisions:

❖ We pay Miklos' expenses plus 15% of the profit on a trip that could last three to four days.

❖ Bill and I would split the profit or the loss.

❖ I will take the two hundred pounds of salt that I picked up from the Russians to exchange for flour from a flour mill close to the Austrian border plus two hundred dollars for expenses and another two hundred dollars for purchase of any product which price is wise and feasible.

❖ We will give twenty dollars to the driver.

Bill told Laci our plan. We had concern over how we could control the driver who had a possible drinking problem. He assured us that we weren't going to have any problems with him. He collected fifty dollars for himself and one hundred dollars for the Russian officer. He would give us a day's advance notice for the trip. On the morning of the trip, he would come with the driver and the truck to our condo and translate any questions we had with the driver and vice versa.

With Miklos, we discussed the preparation for the trip with all the alternatives, including possible separation, injury, arrest by any authority etc. We agreed about the food we were going to carry with us. We had to contact Laci again because we forgot how to handle the driver's food. Laci told us not to worry because the Russian would park and sleep at some Russian post and pick food up there.

Vasil, the driver, had black boots, khaki pants tucked into the boots, shirt, a very lightly stuffed jacket, and a canvas cap. The whole outfit was warm enough for a fall evening outfit, not in freezing cold, snowy weather. During the whole trip, he never buttoned the jacket and only closed the window on his side when he lit a cigarette. He kept the crumpled tobacco leaves in one pocket of his pants, the newspaper in the other. He formed a funnel, filled it up with tobacco (the funnel's open end was at least an inch in diameter), lit up the whole contraption—creating a foot high flame—and could do the whole process with one hand while driving with the other one. He was a happy fellow. Always singing and laughing and often helped carry stuff to and from the truck. He was generously helping us in any way he could.

The First Trip

After loading up the truck with the salt, we said goodbye to everybody and left. The only map we had was two pages from a school book: one for Hungary and one for Austria. Vasil was told by his boss that we were going to Austria. Laci checked out before we left that he had the correct papers including our names and identities. The goal was to go to Vienna. Vasil had his own map but he was familiar with the area because he avoided the main highway and drove on secondary roads. I assumed that secondary roads were less inspected.

The truck definitely wasn't luxury transportation. It wasn't heated—only the motor kept it warm. Every ditch or bump created an orchestra of loose marbles shaken up in a steel bucket. Same the process of changing gears. The cleaning of windows started with a half-gallon of spit cleaned up by crumpled up newspaper. The cab and seats were reasonably clean. Behind us in the cab was a Russian submachine gun hanging from the ceiling holding a round clip of bullets. There were also two full clips on the floor of the cab that were held in place by a dirty, oily rag. The engine was started by a push button. On our side of the cab the window was permanently in the up position. On Vasil's side, the window was moved up or down by pulling the top edge of the window which stayed in position.

The first day was pretty uneventful. We stopped to eat etc. a number of times. Vasil had all kinds of food in his jacket pockets. He could drink large amounts of water. Between driving, smoking, munching, and singing, he pretty much kept himself busy. During the afternoon, we were looking for flour mills to exchange the salt for flour. The locals guided us to an old, old mill. It was late in the afternoon when we arrived at the place and turned into the yard. Two young guys came out. I told them we had two hundred pounds of salt that we would like to exchange for flour and that we were looking for a place to eat and stay for the night.

One of the boys went into the house. Shortly after, the apparent boss came out and introduced himself. He was interested in who we were, what we were there for, and what we had to do with the Russians. After telling him a bunch of lies, he was satisfied and invited us inside. He told us that his mill was a small one and had only a small amount of flour left, and that if we could go to a larger mill about half an hour drive from there, we could probably have a better exchange. We were ready to leave when he asked what kind of exchange we were looking for. I said one pound of salt for every ten pounds of flour. He said it was too much but we could go for one to eight. I said no and told Vasil to go. The boss signaled us to stop. He said he was not changing the one to eight ratio but he would give us dinner and a place to sleep and I okayed it. We received a good dinner and his worker's empty quarters to clean up and sleep.

The next morning, we exchanged the two hundred pounds of salt to two thousand pounds of flour and we went on our way. Vasil was looking for a town which was marked on his map that had a Russian camp to pick up gas. It was very close to the Austrian border. While Vasil was working on his truck, we walked around in the small town to try to find out what was going on across the border. We were told that the Austrian side is pretty much the same as the border area in Hungary. The Austrians come over to shop for food but there was no industrial activity on the other side either.

The flour that we had was bread flour. It was stamped on every sack and also the weight, one hundred pounds. There were twenty sacks. I couldn't believe the exchange rate we got. I have no idea that the salt had such high value. When I originally asked the ten to one ratio, I was bluffing. I am sure in Budapest there was a standard rate for the exchange on the market. The only thing that I had seen when I visited the market was the salt versus flour barter being one of the most popular activity. In the city, salt was used only as a spice, but in the farmland, where every family's major meat source was a minimum of one pig that they butchered in the late fall used salt as a preservative. There wasn't electrical refrigeration in any household in 1945 in Hungary. The four legs and all the bacon were submerged for weeks in a very salty liquid weeks before smoking. Without salt, there was no way to keep large portions of the meat and bacon going into the spring and summer.

It was lunchtime when we reached the border. There was only one Hungarian guard at the Austrian checkpoint, the truck missed it by going back and forth on small roads. We stopped by the first restaurant. We had our first meal of the day. I was looking for the owner and told him what our objective was. He said in the next city there were lots of small businesses.

About thirty kilometers in the direction to Vienna there were a number of businesses which were possibly interested in the flour. At this point, I was mostly concerned for the safety of the whole process and accepted the exchange of a vital food for something valuable as a viable business concept. It wasn't smuggling because neither the Hungarians nor the Austrians could stop Russian military of freely passing the borders carrying anything. The uniqueness about our business was that (1) we had access to cheap and secure transportation, and (2) we had (for the first trip) a critical product in the farmland. We accomplished the easiest part of the business of getting exchangeable product. What was left was finding a buyer who had the product we could sell for dollars back in Hungary.

After reaching the city early in the afternoon, we went from one potential buyer to another. The fourth one was an office equipment and office supply company. This one wasn't open for business (just like the previous ones) but people were cleaning up the place and there were people in the office. I went inside looking for the owner. A middle-aged lady came forward. I told her my story, the twenty bags of flour, the Russian connection, etc. She came out to the truck to check the sacks of flour. She went back to the office and returned telling me that they were interested in the exchange if we could get an agreement. She suggested that we go over to the warehouse and that I should tell her what product I was interested in.

The warehouse was organized, clean and represented a big variety of office products. I asked her how it was possible that the Russians did not clean up the whole contents. She said the Russian troops went through the city real fast. There was no raping and no robbery and the only thing they cleaned out were the wine and liquor. For closing, we established a list and order of preference. The next morning they gave us an offer. They suggested a small restaurant where we could have dinner and breakfast and room to stay overnight. We were a happy group, well-fed and had a good night's sleep. We showered and were ready to go. Back in the main house, we spent a short time to agree. The highlight was ten manual typewriters and a whole list of office supplies from carbon paper to erasers to envelopes to folders.

The biggest problem was protecting shipments from the rain. The truck had a canvas top which belonged to an older truck a long time ago. We received a number of big tarps and Vasil made a perfect job wrapping everything up and then tying the whole mountain together. The next item was to cover the whole thing with firewood that we bought from a neighbor of the warehouse. At goodbye, I asked them if they were interested in a second exchange. They said that they had close to forty employees and they hoped that the amount of flour would last until normal supply was available.

Early next morning we arrived back in Budapest. Vasil was driving with one stop. We unloaded everything in the office, paid Vasil and Miklos, and everybody went home. In the next two weeks we sold everything. The whole trip cleared close to two thousand dollars which we considered was very good—starting with two hundred kilograms of stolen salt.

The Second Trip

Everybody's opinion was that we could make one trip in a month easily. The important thing was that we had to be aware of the changing opportunities between Austria and Hungary and the limited scope of the whole business. The Russian connection can disappear from one day or the next. The border could be closed at any time. This first trip was a lucky coincidence of stolen salt. We agreed to make one more trip with salt. Buying the salt was tricky but we bought four hundred pounds for the second trip. This trip became an overall bummer. We could not get the right kind of exchanges for the salt (we only took two hundred pounds this time and left the other two hundred at home). We ended up exchanging the flour to hardware products of mostly nails, tools like hammers, buckets, and other containers. We sold the nails the first day after returning but got rid of the containers on a loss. We made less than one thousand dollars on the second trip.

The Third Trip

To prepare for the third trip, we agreed to buy everything with dollars and sell all at home for dollars. We were hoping it would speed up the whole transaction. The new buy list included: nails, hammers, handsaws, work shoes, work pants, men's socks, reading glasses, frying pans, petroleum-burning single stoves, lights, etc. Bill and his boss had discussed that their people located a freight train which carried all manufacturing equipment for a glass factory. The boss came to ask me to visit the place (which was thirty miles from the Austrian border on the Hungarian side). We agreed that he would get all the information on the correct location of the train (which was bombed out and sitting in a passing lane) and also provide papers from the Belgian authorities (the factory was Belgian-owned) and papers from the Russians and Hungarians that we could make inventory at the location. In a couple of days the papers arrived, the President gave me five hundred dollars for unexpected expenses then asked me to follow him home (he lived close) because he wanted to speak to me. While going home with him, he asked me what were my plans for the future. I told him that I would try to get a job as a mechanical engineer but that was probably out because of the destruction of the industry. He offered me that when the glass factory would be back in business there were going to be lots of opportunities available. When we arrived at their home, he asked me to come up to the apartment because his wife wanted to speak to me. She was a chemical doctor and spoke four languages and was much younger. She told me that she owned a four-carat diamond ring and that she would like me to sell it when I go to Austria. I told her it is not the right time to run around with a four-carat diamond. I could be picked up by the Russians and the ring would be gone. She said she was aware of it but she thought the American zone in Vienna had to be safe.

The organization of the fourth trip put us at October of 1945. We had the final buy list and the name of the town south of Vienna. The location of our first stop was also the glass factory equipment's location. We had lots of money with us for expenses and buying of the targeted products. As a routine by now, everybody arrived on time. After big goodbyes we were on our way. From the start, we spent most of the time teaching Vasil Hungarian. It was an entertaining program. Vasil enjoyed it. By now he had quite a vocabulary that made all three of our lives simpler. He also translated Russian words to Hungarian while laughing his head off at our pronunciation.

By early afternoon, we arrived at the general area where the glass factory equipment was supposed to be. Locals helped direct us into the direction where the Budapest to Vienna tracks were. It took us two hours to locate the sidetracks where the equipment was which was inside the covered wagons. Each wagon was locked with signs in German and Hungarian that it was Belgian property. We wrote down each wagon's ID number. Next step was to find some railroad personnel on location to find out what would be the future of the long line of railroad cars. We located a railroad track maintenance building and were told that the traffic on the main track was open for months but there was no word about the cars on the side of the tracks. In the beginning of the occupation, it became a "no man's land." I considered the information that we had all what we could have, so we proceeded on our trip.

This trip was complicated by the existence of the division of Vienna into four zones. Vasil was not allowed to go any place outside the Russian zone. We picked up everything we could in two days including a new potential possibility for the future. All three of us were smoking, and in one place where we were loading up blue jeans, the owner of the store asked if we had any cigarettes. He gave us a price list that he would pay for in any volume. We arrived home without any problem and closed the trip with a good profit.

First day at home, I went over to Buda and visited the tobacco factory which was five minutes from my father's condo. When I visited my father, I told him what I was up to, he said one of the foremen in the cigarette production was a good friend of his but he didn't know if he was even alive. He gave me the guy's home address. On the way home, I met his wife. He was working but we agreed I would come back in two days.

My next visit was a successful one because I was told that for an American dollar we could pick up any volume we wanted. He even had prices for different names of cigarettes.

We got in touch with Bill's friend. We explained to him the situation including the fact that we needed a small car because filling up a three-ton truck was just too much of a gamble. The answer was that the price was the same. The car was going to be a 1700's Mercedes with a new driver.

Back at home, we had lots of discussions about how to handle the new situation. The conclusion was that I was going to go alone first because every square inch in the car had to be used to make the business feasible. There was a possible 300% markup and the reason was that the factory sold the cigarettes for Hungarian currency that was in gross inflation versus the dollar. Since we could sell the cigarettes for dollars there was not too much to be concerned about.

Bill's boss, the president of the glass factory, was aware of our new approach so he renewed his interest concerning the diamond ring. He came over with the ring the next day and I didn't have any excuse to turn him down. For me, the whole situation was very uncomfortable. Number one was that he was Bill's boss and two, I considered hiding or protecting the ring during the travel was not a problem, but the boss set the minimum price at five thousand dollars. The diamond was yellow, emerald cut. I was an expert in gold and gold coins as I was buying and selling it but I only had a limited knowledge of diamonds. I bought a lot of gold rings with all kinds of stones and diamonds but we pushed out the stones and given them back to the seller and bought only the gold. The most expensive diamond was the white (clear) diamond with the light blue tint. I had never seen a yellow one before.

The Fourth Trip

On the established day, Bill's friend arrived with the car and the Russian driver. We went over to the tobacco factory to fill up the Mercedes to the top and left.

Vladimir, the new driver, was in his twenties: slim, in good shape, and a good-looking boy. I started out with the bridge building sign

71

language and after a few hours he apparently got tired of it and with fluent German asked what my profession is. This was a big surprise. He told me that in the very beginning of the war, he was captured by the Germans and worked as a mechanic in a German factory. When the Russians captured the factory, he was sent back to his original outfit which was located in Budapest. He was a Russian officer but was demoted to a soldier without rank because he was captured by the Germans.

We arrived the same night at Vienna and looked up Ludwig (he was the guy who suggested the cigarette business). He was very happy with the cigarettes we bought and invited us for dinner. He offered a room in his warehouse where we could sleep in but I turned it down because I intended to return to Budapest early in the morning. This was only an excuse because I still had the diamond to deal with. We unloaded the cigarettes, picked up the money, and were about to go when Ludwig asked me to visit his neighbor because he wanted to talk to me. The neighbor suggested buying used cars from him and he gave me a list of cars and papers he could supply. He had no papers for the cars but all of them were in working condition. He needed two weeks notice.

Leaving Ludwig, we settled down in a small "guest house." I bought a bottle of wine and some cheese. Vladimir told me stories of his life in German captivity. I had a shower and slept like a bear. Next morning, we were looking for a jewelry store but were told there are none in the Russian zone. I left Vladimir in a Russian base and went over to the American zone to find a jewelry store. The jeweler took one look at the ring and shook his head. "Nobody would buy a yellow diamond in Vienna," was the verdict. That was enough for me. I went back to join Vladimir. He was ready to go. I had the money behind the trunk liner to secure passing Russian inspection, and by nightfall, we were back in Hungary.

This latest possibility of selling cigarettes for dollars was the most efficient and fastest way to conduct business. We could have Miklos or me stationed in Vienna and let Vladimir drive back and forth. To combine this with buying cars was an interesting potential that

I was going to investigate. In the meantime, Christmas was getting closer. Miklos and Vladimir made one more trip and we closed the year. Bill, Miklos, and I made money. The Russians were not complaining. Bill's boss still had his ring and overall, all of us were satisfied.

The year 1946 started with my investigation of the car market in Budapest. Comparing potential sale prices in Budapest and Vienna, the markup was more than double. The reason was that all the cars which were in running condition were confiscated by Russians; and the reorganization of the political parties and some of the state's or the city's administration created a seller's market for cars.

I sent Miklos with the first cigarette shipment back to Vienna. Also he was to locate a car that we could purchase and a car repair shop that can check out the car so that we do not end up with a lemon. He should work with Ludwig's friend who suggested the car program.

The Fifth Trip

The next question was if we can get support from the Russians to drive one of the newly purchased cars. Ludwig's friend told me that the different car models for which prices he quoted were without papers, meaning, they were stolen from somebody. He also suggested that most of the cars were probably German army cars, abandoned by Austrian and German soldiers who quit the German army after reaching Austria. We (Bill and I) had a meeting with Bill's friend to get answers of the specific question: whether the Russians can provide papers for the car to drive back from Vienna to Budapest. We would have the car readied once Vladimir arrived back in Vienna so the second driver could make the trip in one day.

A week later, Bill's friend came back with the answer: price of $250 upwards, need two weeks' notice.

The Seventh Trip

The weather was very bad. It was the end of January. I was preparing to pick up the cigarettes for the next trip when I realized that I had to go with Vladimir to Vienna to make sure that the first car program was prepared by Miklos. Understanding what had to be accomplished, we had to wait until the first of February or until the weather cleared out before I leave for Vienna.

After arriving, the cigarette sales were finished in an hour. I told Vladimir to cool his heels for three to four hours before we could go back. I brought Miklos up to date concerning the car program. To start out, he had to purchase a car. The preferred model was a Mercedes, a small four-door car. Then he had to get the specified information that the Russians needed for their paperwork and send it back to us, etc. In the meantime, we visited Ludwig's friend Herman, the car dealer. He had a 2200 Mercedes and a Horch. Both were too big of a car for the Hungarian market. I never heard of Horch before. It was a luxury sedan. The driver was separated from the passenger compartment by a glass divider. The passenger area had one folding seat. According to Ludwig, Hitler's cars were all Horchs. The price was unbelievably cheap because of the association to Hitler, so I decided to buy it because in Hungary there was no association. The car was in excellent condition. It was black and very impressive. After I had all the data, we returned to Hungary to get the Russian started and to get the Horch back to Budapest.

March 1946

It was March when the car finally arrived. It became a major headache. We parked it in the Butcher family's warehouse. We were afraid to drive it because the Russians may confiscate it. Nobody wanted it because of the luxury size and appearance. I was trying to get a diplomatic license when I met a Chinese diplomat named Cheng who was living with his Hungarian girlfriend in a small hotel. He said he was just lately transferred from Italy to Hungary. He had no problem getting a diplomatic license plate. He wanted to see the car and fell in love with it. He bought it in the blink of an eye. We became good friends until one day he disappeared with his girlfriend and the car. The rumor was that in private, he was a film producer and went back to Italy.

We managed to buy and sell two 1700 Mercedes when Vladimir brought the news that Miklos was taken by the police. We found out that Austrian authorities arrested him for smuggling, put him in jail, and let him out after three months. When he returned, he said he had $1100 in cash when he was arrested. The Austrian authorities confiscated the money. We did not see him for a long time. I was the engineering manager of a structural steel company in 1954 when I visited a large industrial site in Hungary that I ran into Miklos. He was the manager of the complex's restaurants. He was in good shape; he had a five year old girl.

* * *

This happened during our smuggling time. My friend and I were walking in the American sector speaking Hungarian when an American officer stopped us. He said he was a medical doctor back in Cleveland. His parents immigrated to the United States. He offered to sit down with us for a drink. We were happy to accept. It was late afternoon. We went into an American officer's club and sat down at the bar. We ordered wine while he ordered beer. Right next to me was a great big American officer who just received his order of beer, ketchup, and egg. To my big surprise, he broke the raw egg and poured it into the beer, then the ketchup, then lots of salt and black pepper and started drinking it. I can still see the egg floating in his beer. I asked the doctor about it, he said he had never seen anybody drinking a similar concoction. After living in the United States, I heard that some people prepared their beer that way.

Nationalization

It started with the big, large industries and major corporations. In the meantime, the owners of the midsized companies felt lucky and satisfied that their biggest headache was nationalized, never thinking that they were going to be next.

The smaller companies, like mine, were the last ones. Many just closed and were eliminated. Like mine, others combined with the same kind to a size that was more controllable.

This is how my business started:

After the smuggling business, I was ready to work for a job when Bill's boss asked me to see him. He was very friendly and told me that I could have an engineering job at the glass plant, but I told him I intended to stay in Budapest. Then he told me that once the factory was working, he could suggest to all the glass wholesalers to use the putty made by me. It was a sure business since he was the only sheet glass manufacturer in Hungary.

The putty was the substance which held the glass in the window frame. I was really surprised about his help and told him that owning my own business was a dream for me. Looking into the details, I discovered that a special vegetable oil was one of the components for the putty and that it is in short supply and its availability questionable in the volume I needed.

I did not have to discuss that with the boss when he told me he wanted to see me. He said one of the largest glass wholesale owners in Budapest died during the war and his widow did not intend to continue business and was looking for somebody to take it over with her retaining some partial ownership. That was for me like winning the lottery. The lawyers put the legalities in order and by time the glass production started, it was ready for business. It was initially a distribution place, not a business, since window glass was, and will be in short supply for years to come. The boss gave me a large allotment based on the past history of the company and I have to sell it to installers.

In the meantime, my son Pete was born as the first extension of the Zak name. Both mother and child were in good shape and healthy. It was September 1946.

The country was slowly recovering from WWII and more and more got under the influence of the Communist Party. The division of Europe, that was originally perceived to be temporary, ended up permanent and Hungary became part of the eastern bloc, not under the influence of Russia but under the dictatorship of Russia.

The business was a goldmine. It provided an excellent lifestyle but also the fast accumulation of cash. I started installing glass for some storefronts—it was a second goldmine. The handling of large pieces of glass was a special occupation and we had the people who had the experience.

In normal times, a business like this would go from generation to generation and the owners were rich people. Instead of this, on December 27, 1949, three men walked into my office, two civilian and one policeman. The two were dressed in a typical blue-collar outfit. One of them gave me an unopened envelope and told me to open it up. The official paper was addressed to me telling me that my glass wholesale business was taken over by the government and that I should follow the two men's instructions.

I couldn't remove anything from the business and I also had to turn over my car. The order's effective time: right that instant. I asked if I could tell my employees what happened, they said they would take care of everything. I went for my winter coat but they said I leave it. The policeman told them that I could take the coat. They asked for my car keys. I gave it to them. I picked up my gloves from the car and left. Later the same day, I looked up the place. It was closed and remained closed for years. Years later a friend from France visited. I told him the story and he said, "Why didn't you call the police?"

Commercial Police

The commercial police investigated any real or false wrongdoing. I became a victim of this organization. My business was nationalized in 1949. Two weeks after my business was nationalized I was picked up by two detectives of the commercial police. The charge was that I cheated on my income tax. I was only in business for three years and every year an authorized accountant checked out my books and prepared a tax return that I submitted to our lawyer who then submitted it to the government. The detectives' office was on the second floor of the commercial police central building. When we first sat down in the interrogation room and the detective listed the charges against me, I knew it was the beginning of a large fishing expedition. The detective was a young guy, my age and very businesslike. I do not believe his education went beyond eighth grade. From that day on, every morning from eight o'clock to five o'clock, six days a week and for the next eight weeks, I was investigated by the same detective.

I never knew whether that day or the next day they would beat me up or keep me locked up. One day the detective said not to come the following day. I thought it was finished, but I soon realized I was wrong. About a month later, I got an official order that on a given day a judge will adjudicate my case. I had three months to prepare to defend against the charges which were all bogus, and I had witnesses to prove it. The question was, would the witnesses back up my case or were they instructed by the commercial police to lie? I had mixed feelings.

When I was originally picked up by the police, it was reported in every newspaper. After that, I started noticing that my old and new friends kept away from me to the extent that some of them would cross the street to walk on the sidewalk on the other side of the street rather than come near me.

I hired my old high school friend who became a lawyer to represent me. The day of the trial was cold and with many dark clouds. This was not a good sign if you are superstitious, which I am. My lawyer was there, but only for support since I was representing myself. The judge wanted to know why I did this. I told him there were too many allegations and I am more familiar with each of them. The case was presented by the government lawyer and when it was my turn, I started going from one allegation to the next, explaining my side. I was at the third allegation when the judge interrupted the proceedings and closed the case saying I was innocent and that I could leave. I knew I was innocent but a full pardon was something I did not expect. The bailer told me he never had a similar situation before. He had cases with good endings but not by interrupting and closing the case. This was also the year I got divorced. Later, I married again.

My Brother

My brother was in the building trade, supervising construction projects. He was invited to visit the celebration of a completed project that he started. At the time, he was working in Budapest. One night, I received a call from a lawyer from a town west of Budapest about fifty miles from the Austrian border. He told me that my brother had been arrested for trying to escape from Hungary. Upon arriving at the jail, he hired a lawyer to represent him. The lawyer did not know the details and the case would go before a judge in two months. He wanted to know if I would pay for his work. We agreed on a fee and I paid half before, and half after the trial. The lawyer said that the jail visitation was on the first weekend of every month.

My wife and I visited him at the first opportunity. It was summer and we met him in the jail yard. We brought him a package of food and cigarettes that the guard checked out, putting one pack of cigarettes in his pocket. My brother looked OK. I asked him what happened. He said after arriving, they had a big dinner and told lots of stories but my brother had to leave early to catch the train going back to Budapest. He got on the train early and was happy that he got there early because he had a few too many drinks and didn't want to go home drunk. He fell asleep, and the next thing he knew a border policeman was waking him up and asking for his passport. He said he did not have one and asked why he would need a passport. Apparently, he took the wrong train that is headed westbound to Austria rather than the Budapest to the east. He went to jail but was not worried because the jail was in the same town as the celebration was and a number of people could verify that he had no reason to leave the country. He was just drunk.

The date of the trial came. The lawyer called up to say that my brother was free and should be back in two days after the paperwork was finalized. Two days, and later a week came and went with no brother. I called the lawyer and he said he had no idea what happened because the judge released my brother. A week later, we finally heard from my brother and he said we should come visit him because he was in jail in another town. We visited him and he told us that after the trial he went back to the jail to wait to be released. Instead he was presented with a paper admitting he intended to leave the country. He said he was just found not guilty and he would not sign anything. They said that they had all the time in the world and if he signed the paper he would only serve two years. He signed the paper.

From Boss Back to Employment

In the communist world, formerly owning a nationalized business was like looking for a job without being able to read or write. I was looking for any manual job without luck. Finally, I ran into one of my high school classmates who was a group leader in a large lumber yard and they needed warehouse workers. He said he made an arrangement to introduce me to his boss and he was sure he was going to hire me because they are looking for more than one worker. Two days later I was hired. I was walking to a bus to go home when I passed an office just one block from the lumberyard with a sign on the office window looking for a draftsman. I went in. It was a structural steel company. It did not tell them I was an engineer but a draftsman. They hired me and I start working at eight the next day. The engineering department had one engineer and six draftsmen. The whole office, from bookkeeping to processing, were mostly former military officers, former government workers, small business owners, etc. It was a great group and my salary was good. So it was a lucky find.

My job was simple but interesting. In a year, I became project engineer. Typically I had two to three projects running at the same time all supporting the production of steel components for new industrial or commercial businesses.

In the middle of the second year, the head of the engineering department gave me the specification for a warehouse of a tobacco fermenting company. There was a special interest to read the specification of each part and the basic rough drawing. Each part called out the dimensions but there were no details of the parts. We had designed the details of the part and submitted the design to the architectural designer of the whole building. There were nine items in the project, eight of them were different steel doors. The last one were storage shelves that ran on wheels, having five shelves with trays, five on each shelf that in turn ran on ball bearings in and out of the shelves. After reading all the information on the fermenting room, it became clear there was no need for ball bearings as regular hardened bearing would do the job. I immediately called the person in charge and told him that I had a plan that could bring about substantial savings. He came over and documented my suggestion.

It was an important rule in the socialist order that if anybody had a money savings suggestion, the person will receive ten percent of one year savings in cash. I ended up with about two years worth of salary in cash. Not just that, but also fame and promotion to a higher position.

The Old Factory

The company where I was transferred had six other structural companies under its direction. Three of the companies were located in Budapest, four were all over Hungary. Their trust in me promoted me to another company in Budapest.

Many workers in the shop worked for the old company, and so were the women in the office. There I became the engineering manager—head of a small department with two engineers, two technicians, and six draftsmen. According to the old-timers, the original company had five hundred workers and forty people in office. By the time I got there in 1951, the shop still had five hundred workers but there were over 120 people in the office.

In the old company, there was one president and a secretary. In the new company, the president's office had: the president, two secretaries, one driver and one programmer. Then there was the Communist Party office with six people, while the union had four. The old company had one engineer, the new one, one chief engineer, me, and my group which had two more. Then we also had one purchasing guy who was replaced by a department of seven; time study, thirty-one; time study documentation, sixty-four; warehouse, three; gate guys, four; health, two; and vacation, accounting, maintenance, ten.

The workweek in the office was six days, five days with eight to five hours of work with half an hour unpaid lunchtime and on

Saturdays, eight to one thirty, for a total of forty-eight hours. The factory had the same hours of work only they started an hour earlier and went home an hour earlier. Saturday was the day off for the factory workers. The office workers had fixed monthly salaries and were paid twice a month. The factory workers were paid every week but their income was based on performance. The job that they have to perform had a price—the simplest job—sweeping the factory floor. They were paid, for example, ten cents, to sweep one hundred square feet. Our plant was one hundred thousand square feet. The whole plant was worth one hundred dollars but it took three people every day to sweep the one hundred thousand square feet to make thirty-three dollars a day.

When the whole process was originally introduced, everybody was paid hourly. They timed each sweeper to establish how many square feet they have to sweep per hour. Naturally, people worked slowly being afraid that they have to work very hard when piecework was established. Instead the norm was based on slow performance. It took the factory six months to develop norms for most of the operations. Everybody was making good money. They said this is paradise. Then they cut the wage to fifty percent. It was a disaster. The management said it is a trial. But it was never changed. However, there were workers who under the new norm could double the output of others. They became the heroes.

One thing was not tolerated, skipping a day of work for any reason, especially drinking. If it was repeated too often by a person, he was picked up from home by the police and taken to a detox facility. On the first day, people were invited to a room full with every possible alcohol on the table. They were served food and allowed to drink as much as they wanted. Then for the next two weeks, they put them on medication and repeat the same offering of alcohol. At the first day, nobody can touch it as the sight of booze makes them sick.

The story was told to me by a welder who was famous about the amount of hard liquor he could drink. We'd get together in a local bar after work on Fridays. It was an unwritten rule that the office people went for a drink in the same bar to show solidarity with the workers. This is how I got friendly with the welder.

One morning he didn't show up for work, so the secretary of the union went to his house to pick him up. Because he was a very good welder, he was delinquent enough to be taken to detoxification. This is how the secretary told me the story: He rang the doorbell to his apartment. His wife came out and opened the door to let him in. Inside on a couch the welder was sleeping stark naked. She said that he came home around midnight. He hardly could walk, and when she opened the door, the welder stopped before the door, took all his clothes off and gave it to the guy who took him home. He drank his clothing and, according to his wife, he didn't have anything left to wear.

He went for detox, came home, and didn't drink for six months. The next time I saw him he was holding himself to a lamppost—drunk. I asked him how long he was drinking. "Only the last couple days," he said. "You know it was pretty hard, but I was working on it and finally made it."

It was a cold winter when they found him dead by the bus station one morning frozen to death.

In a communist country, you don't pay tax. Only the people who still had their own business paid taxes and some doctors, artists, actors, etc.

The communist economy was based on consecutive five-year plans. Budget was given to each of the major departments yearly. This was broken down to each of the chapter of the department then to each company in the chapter. The companies all received what they had produced during a year and based on this information the company's performance was supervised during the year. The first day of the new plan was introduced with a big celebration and everybody was asked to "offer" a sum for his or her contribution during the year which was deducted from every paycheck.

Our company was the largest of the seven supervised by a trust. My job was that if a company wasn't performing to the standards, I was sent over to straighten them out. One of the first one was about fifty miles from Budapest. When I arrived, the local president found me a place to stay. It was the local teacher's house. My room was comfortable and clean. He was accommodating.

I had to stay there for two weeks. It was also a nationalized company with two hundred people. The president was foreman in the old company. I was observing and taking notes for three days. On the fourth day, I sat down with the president to tell him what my observation was. I told him I was not there to listen why they were doing so many things wrong. There were no exceptions to my rules—if somebody wasn't performing, the worker does not get a warning but immediate deduction of his base hourly rate for three months. He held a meeting the same afternoon about morning arrival time, strict lunchtime, no story telling etc.

All the products that they made they collected in a large grassy area. They were all painted red to protect them from rust. Most of them were steel doors of different sizes. The first hour I arrived I noticed twelve doors which were probably five feet high and two feet wide. All had a small steel window about three feet high.

Close to the end of my two-week stay, the president came to me to tell me he was going to a building site because there were some problems. I told him I would go with him. When we arrived to the building site, we drove to the office. A middle-aged guy with a beard greeted us. He was the manager of the construction. We told him the reason for our visit. He had a big smile on his face. "You have to see that," he said. We walked back to the building. It was made of concrete. We went to the basement. In the center of the basement there was a wide corridor, on one side there was a line of showers and on the other side there were twelve doors that I was wondering about back in the shop because of the small size. We passed them and ended up on the other side of the building where there were stairs going up making a right turn to the next floor. On the basement floor, there was the rail welded up from a good-sized tubing. The problem was that the rail made a left turn instead of a right like the stairs. This made all three of us laughed. There was no doubt about it, it had to be returned and corrected.

As we were walking back passing before the doors again, I opened one door and looked behind. The "room" was a little more than two feet by two feet with a high ceiling with a great big lightbulb in the center. I asked the construction manager what was the purpose, thinking it was some industrial application. He made a face and said, "This is going to be a secret police building. They will keep people in this room whom they want to convince whatever they did was not "practical." The only thing that you can do in the place is to stand up. You couldn't sit, turn, kneel, nothing."

Land without Reform

The Russian military operation was completed in April of 1945. From that moment on, the political parties started to organize. The three major parties were the Small Holders' Party, the Social Democratic Party, and the Communist Party. The Communist Party didn't exist since the end of WW I when the Communists ruled the country for four months. The first election was held in 1945 when the Communists received 17% of the vote. The country was transformed from democracy to communist dictatorship by 1948. Almost anything—the law, social order, the religion, the industry, the business, the economy, the private life, etc., did not exist anymore or changed to something unrecognizable.

Before the Russian occupation, people left Hungary by the thousands. Universities, government offices, military, families and factories were officially moved to the West. Heads of large corporations, big landowners, rich people, and ordinary people afraid from the Russian left on their own. Most of them remained in the West forever, only a small portion returned. After returning, everybody had to face a small group of people assembled on last place, the person worked to investigate their political history during the German occupation of Hungary. The judgment was based on the controlling group's opinion that was very forgiving. It was still a scary procedure. The early election in 1945 gave everybody hope for a democratic future, especially after the Communist received only 17% of the vote.

The land reform was accomplished in 1945. Before the war, 86% of the land was owned by small farmers, 10% by Catholic churches, and 4% by aristocrats. The land of the churches and aristocrats and also of large landowners were distributed to small farmers and farmworkers who didn't own land. That was the first time in my memory that the state confiscated privately owned properties without compensation. I didn't know the history of the Catholic Church and how and when they received their land but it must be part of some grant of favor from the kingdom.

In the next three to four years, a big portion of the land was organized into cooperatives and ruined by low output and quality of the inefficient bureaucracy of multiple ownership of the land. Members of the cooperatives received compensation based on their common efforts. The state had provided the seed and fertilizers and also the equipment to prepare and harvest the land. During the year, all this outside help was charged against the cooperative, and by the end of the year, deducted for from the income that resulted in unending fight between all involved.

I was a "city" boy and absolutely unfamiliar with the people and life on the farm. My wife's family owned a small vacation home on the shore of a large lake fifteen to thirty miles from Budapest. It was very a primitive place with two rooms and a kitchen. They purchased it before the war, and by the time I joined the family, it was leased to a young family with three children. The husband was a watchman for the surrounding privately owned vineyards. During the summer months, we spent the weekend in one room.

I absolutely loved the place, the town, the lake, the small vineyards on the hills. The house was located on a narrow lot and had a small level area on the street side. The rest went downhill to the water. The level area was where the house was located. Next to the house was an open well—round, about fifty feet deep, with two feet of rim around it, and a hand operated shaft with rope. On the rope was a standard bucket placed just above the water. It took twenty or so cranks to get the water up. Water was always real cold. In the summer, a watermelon or cantaloupes were placed in the bucket to cool. In the far side of the level part of the lot was an outhouse. The bottom of the door was about ten inches above the ground to show if it was occupied.

There was a large mulberry tree by the house. The berries were the size of a cherry, dark purple and very sweet. There was also a large chicken coop housing a whole army of chickens, geese, and ducks. Every year when the mulberries were ripe, lots of them fell to the ground and only the ducks ate them. The ducks could not keep up as so many of them fell on the ground. On the hot summer, it fermented, and the ducks loved it to the point that by the night, all of them got drunk. They could not walk and just laid on their backs with their legs up pumping in the air.

The chickens were always around the house. The ducks and geese were let off every morning to the lake and rounded up at night. There was an open water area about ten houses wide. Every house had twenty to thirty geese and ducks. To collect the geese was a remarkable process. There was a fence and a gate at the end of the lot. When late afternoon arrived, the ducks gathered on their own by their own gate. The geese remained in the water until Mariska went to the shore and yelled li-li, li-li. Her group of geese was flying to the gate. There were a lot of geese belonging to the houses on the shore. Some of them were feeding on the water in the cattail plants while others swim around the water. When Mariska started bellowing, only her geese answered the call.

The house was also something different. It was about eight hundred square feet with three rooms and wooden steps going to the attic. The house was built with mud, the roof was cottontail. One summer, they were building a new house next door. On, the first day, they laid out the blueprint of the house. The wall was about two feet thick. Then they started picking up dirt, clay, and straw, and made a mixture of all these by adding water to it until it became a wet mud (with the straw in big clumps all over). Then they got a horse and let the horse walk over it for four to five hours until the whole mixture was mixed together evenly. It took them two weeks to reach the full height of the house using six by six wood and wood panels for the ceiling or the flooring of the attic. Then they erected the structure for the roof. The roof was cottontail which was hand-laid starting from the bottom. The final roof was about ten inches thick of cottontail. The cottontail was cut with a special tool when the lake was frozen.

The flooring of the house was also mud mixed with straw. The entry of the house was going into the kitchen. The ceiling of the kitchen was half round with a large square hole in the cent for the chimney. The kitchen stove had a short chimney for the smoke from the stove going to the chimney. The chimney was also serving as a smokehouse. Every family had one or more pigs during the year and killed it in the early part of winter. The hams, bacon, etc., were hung inside the chimney for smoking.

The whole town had three hundred homes, a Catholic and a Presbyterian church, school level of up to eight grade, two grocery stores. There was no physician and had up to one vegetable garden acre around the house. Three to ten of those acres were mostly devoted to raising corn. Probably half of the town owning one cow gathered every morning to spend all day on the pasture and got home by night. The pigs spent the whole week on the pasture and returned for the weekend. They both find their own homes, never making a mistake.

The land reform did not influence anybody in the town. Everybody was under the maximum 140-acre limit. During the years, they changed the upper limit to forty acres, still no problem. The people got by year to year with the small land that they had. Everybody owned their home or vineyard. The pigs, ducks, geese, and chicken provided them with plenty of food and the small cash they needed came from selling dairy products and wine.

They generally know their limitation and were a happy bunch. We regularly started going down there after 1949 when my business was nationalized. Communism hardly changed anything concerning their lifestyle. Once the kids went to bed every Saturday night, we got a full report of what was going on in the town and at home.

Problem with the animals, etc. The weekends and the tranquility of the small town kept us going.

The hilly country, the lake, the small acreage per family saved the area from land reform. The nationalized area of the country lost its high productivity by the disorganized bureaucrats in control. Hungary was called before the war as the "breadbasket of Europe" because of exportations of big portions of its agricultural products. During the communist time, it hardly could support home consumption. Not just the volume went down but also the quality.

In peace, the potato was washed clean. In communist time, it was sold with a good portion of dirt. Lining up for grocery was a common site in Budapest. Meat was available only once a week, that is, Saturday morning. You have to line up three to four hours for two pounds of meat, no more than two eggs at one time, and with hardly any milk product, and on and on.

Health insurance was for Budapest bureaucrats only. Doctors made house calls. The possible reason was that the people needed a doctor's help only when the home medication cannot help anymore and the person was in bed. Doctors ordered medication in most cases which were custom mixed by the drugstore. There was no such thing as yearly check-ups for preventative care.

The other remarkable thing in town was that all the work in the house, the yard around the house, the land on the vineyard was performed by no machine. Everything was done by hand and tools. There was one exception: the land was plowed using horses. The hoe was used to clean the weeds in vineyards and in the cornfield. Vegetables were collected by hand, fruits picked by hand, so were the grapes, etc. Wheat were cut with sickle, bunched up for carrying by hand. But seeds were separated by (the only machine in agriculture). There was also machine in the kitchen: a meat grinder for sausage. There were winter get-together for the ladies. Shucking corn and separating the stem of the geese feather for down covers. The whole family had to be in good shape and healthy to keep going.

The Police

The police in Budapest disappeared during the first few months of the occupation by the Russians. The only visible Hungarian organization was the Red Cross. Their numbers were growing because they represented protection, especially for the men, because the Russians were continually picking up military-aged men for labor camps. There was a rumor that the Russian generals needed people as an alibi for the months of combat to occupy the city which was protected by a small number of German and Hungarian soldiers. The other protection the Red Cross offered was that it gave people an identification card written in Russian saying that the person holding the card was a foreigner. I received one from my father's Russian friends stating that I was working in a hospital. The Russian soldiers that were asking for identification studied everything that was written on an identification document, but it was all for show because they were all illiterate.

After many months, Hungarian police became finally visible. First, they took over traffic control from the Russians then keeping peace and order. The police were also the first line recipients of communist complaints from snitches. There were armies of snitches, and they would allow this to defenders of the communist rules but not rewarded by the party with lucrative jobs. They were reporting the smallest infraction of communist rules, sending thousands of innocent people to brutal interrogation and hard labor camps.

The best example was my wife's cousin. She was a hardworking twenty-year-old married lady who was working for a foundry. During lunch discussions, she made a statement that every politician is a crook. The next day she was picked up by the police. She could not deny what she said because there were a lot of people in the lunchroom who heard the comment. They did not touch her because she was pregnant but they did send her to a labor camp where she was picking cotton and working in the hot sun. She miscarried the baby in the field. Her luck was that there was a lady doctor working nearby. She gave her medical assistance and took care of her properly.

The Secret Police

The secret police was the most horrifying organization of the communist order. No one knew who the head of it was and it was hardly ever mentioned in any news. Its headquarters was in the Budapest area. The following will give you an idea of their methods.

I woke up to the sound of the doorbell and ran to open the door when a voice said *police*. It was 2:00 a.m. The door was pushed against me so hard that I fell on my back. I stood up, facing two men in their thirties dressed in dark suits, one telling me to dress up because I was coming with them. When I was dressed, I was led to a small car with a driver and was told to sit in the backseat. When I asked where we were going, I was told that I would see. We were driving south through Budapest. It was raining but the roads were well lit. We passed downtown and took a bridge over the Danube River and turned south again. Then the driver turned left and stopped in front of a large steel door.

I knew the building and the whole area. It was a ten-minute walk from my parents' condo where I grew up. A soldier with a Russian submachine gun hanging from his shoulder opened the gates. The building was a military garrison covering the whole city block. It was one story high all around with few windows facing the outside. In the past, nobody knew what was going on inside the building or what the military purpose of it was. There was very little traffic going in and out of the steel gate and there was never a guard on the outside of the gate. The windows facing the outside were always lit at night and so was the large interior of the complex.

The three of us left the car and went inside the building. It was a long corridor before us, one that ran the full length of the building. It was about twelve feet wide with green doors on both sides. There were wood benches placed on one side. Without speaking one word, we went to the far end of the corridor and stopped at a bench. They told me to sit down and then went inside a room facing the bench. At that point of my life was not worth a single cent. I had friends and relatives who were picked up at night and disappeared forever. Parents, kids, and relatives did not know who to turn to for information. Only very few of them were told where they could pick up the body. Also a few of them released two or three years later with stories that were hard to believe.

After waiting there for about an hour, I was asked to come inside what appeared to be an office. It was a small room with two desks and a couple of chairs. A military officer was sitting behind one desk. The two guys were nowhere to be seen. The officer asked me to sit down, and took out a yellow sheet of paper with my name printed on the top. He asked me all kinds of questions—beginning with simple information like my address and then moving on to things like why did I attend college in Germany. Finally he told me that in the next room there were going to be people lined up and that I had to go in front of them—no rush—and very carefully look at every one of them. I was to tell him if I knew or had seen any of them before. I had to walk once in front of them and turn around at the end of the line and walk behind their backs. There were two guards in the room watching. There had to be no communication between me and the prisoners and my hand was to be at my side with fingers stretched out. No coughing or scratching my throat. I had to repeat every instruction to the officer.

The officer opened the door and walked behind me. There were thirty or forty people lined up in one row dressed in pants and shirts and sweaters. All of them were badly beaten. Their eyes and faces were black and blue and had healing cuts on their head. One guy's ear was swollen to the size of a large potato. Their clothing was hanging on them as a sign of weight loss. Nobody was clean and several of them had bandages on their hands or other places.

I slowly walked in front of them searching for faces. When I reached the end of the line, one of the guards pointed at me to make a turn to the back of the line. Walking behind, the only thing I could see was that a few of them had injuries on the neck or head. After I finished the inspection, the officer directed me to go back to the office and told me to wait outside. I waited again close to an hour. When I was told to come in and sit down, he reached for my yellow sheet and asked me if I saw anyone I knew to which I said no. He asked if I knew why they were beaten and I said I really didn't know, and that if I had to guess, they must have committed some kind of crime like robbery or assault or something really bad. He wanted to know if I noticed that they were all skinny and I said I did not because I was too much absorbed in looking at their faces.

He wrote down all of my answers then told me to go back and repeat the observation. I went back and only noticed one thing: they were all lined up in the same order as they were before. The officer told me to go out again and wait. After five or ten minutes, a soldier came out of the office and told me to follow him. We went back to the steel gates in which he opened a small door and told me that I could leave.

It was pitch-dark outside. The street lights were turned off. It was a cold, wet November morning. I found an old cigarette in my coat pocket but no lighter—an appropriate end to the experience.

* * *

Three brothers lived in the same apartment building that I grew up in. The youngest one was three or four years older than me. I know he was educated to become an accountant. The middle one and I did not know too much about him other than that he played at the same tennis club I did during my high school years. The oldest one was captain when I was eight or ten years old. I knew him better than the other two. He liked my father, and many times he came over to our condo on weekday nights to play cards with my father and friends. He was a celebrity among our friends not just because he was a captain but also because he was a pilot and always had some military or flying story. After I left for Germany to go to college, I lost touch with the brothers. The war and the Russian occupation really dispersed people all over the map. Many people left because they were afraid of the Russians and many people had to move because the bombing destroyed their homes. The side of the condo where the three brothers lived collapsed from continuous artillery fire, but they were gone by then.

About two years later at the end of the war, I ran into the youngest brother while walking in the neighborhood. I barely had a chance to say hello when he started telling me that his older brother also served in the Air Force during the war just like his captain brother. Both ended up in Germany by the end of the war and both returned safely to Budapest. The captain became a colonel over the years and became one of the few who was hired back in the new army after the occupation. About three weeks before I ran into the youngest brother, the two older brothers were picked up at night and ever since no one in the family had heard anything about them. Three months later, I heard from a friend that they were both executed. When I looked up about the youngest brother, neither he nor any close relatives had any information.

One day months and months later, I was sitting at a café when I saw the colonel buying a newspaper on the street. I ran out to greet him but he had a hard time recognizing me. We gave each other a hug and returned back to the café together. He told me that after they were picked up, he never saw his brother until he was released.

He was recovering at home when his brother was released a week later. He survived the brutal interrogation that accused him of treason. When the investigation was finished, he moved to another prison awaiting sentencing. He was there for two and a half months before he was released. When he was home for about a month, the younger brother was picked up at night. He said nobody heard anything about him ever since. This was 1950. I left Budapest on the fall of 1956 and he was still missing.

* * *

My older cousin was eight years older than me. He and his father had a restaurant. My grandfather owned an inn. My grandfather owned an inn (100 years ago). My cousin and his father kept up the tradition by staying in the restaurant business. In the forties, he owned a small restaurant in the suburbs of Budapest at the end of the city rail line. His restaurant was nationalized in 1949 just like mine, but they let him run the restaurant. He had one helper. He was selling mostly wine and beer, no hot food, just sandwiches that were fixed by his second wife. When I had my car I visited him a lot. He was a great big guy, not fat just muscle.

We were in the United States when he died. We did not know the circumstances of his death. It was 1958 and I had only my brother left in Hungary. The only way we could communicate was by telephone—which was very seldom—but mostly with letters. My brother never mentioned our cousin in the letters. My brother lost connection with our cousin's wife and it was probably ten years after his death that I realized I never heard what caused his death. I asked my brother to look into it.

He found my cousin's wife. She told him that he was still working in the small restaurant when he was picked up by the secret police. He had two friends who visited the restaurant practically daily. According to the secret police, they were spies. They suspected that my cousin knew about them. His wife got a telephone call two weeks after he was arrested saying that he was in a local hospital having problems with his eye. He had been beaten so badly that he could not see. He died two weeks later in the hospital.

* * *

My wife's uncle was a colonel and a military judge in the army before World War II. After the war was over, he was called back to the army and was told to swear to the new flag. He refused, saying that he swore to a flag once and he was not going to swear to a different flag. A year later, he was called back and offered the job of military attaché in England. His guess was that the reason for this exceptional offer was, first, he had a law degree and spoke three different languages and second, before World War II, he was assigned to organize and carry out a Hungarian communist prisoner exchange with the Russians. The prisoners became the leading communists in Hungary after World War II. He rejected the offer because of his poor health although actually, he was in his mid-fifties and in excellent health.

Months later, he was picked up by the secret police. He was set free after six months, a time during which no one knew where he was. He was not recognizable. He had lost lots of weight, he could hardly walk, and his whole body was bruised up. He was told he was accused of treason for organizing a military uprising. He was tortured daily. He did not want to go into details, but years later, he said that one of the tortures was that they took him from his basement cell in the morning and took him up to the third floor. There they put his legs up to the knee in a bucket with crushed ice and changed the ice often. At the end of the day, they ordered him to walk back to his cell. He couldn't walk. They kicked him from the third floor down to the basement. It took him two days to recover and then they started again. It took his wife six months to get him back to normal but never back to where he was before the arrest. He became an old man in his late fifties.

Around this time, the Communists organized a big exodus of people who were not trusted by the communist regime. There were thousands of people. Each person was ordered to leave Budapest and give the name of the town where they were supposed to go. Most of them ended up in empty barns and empty storage places supported by the people in the town and visiting relatives.

The Ruling Class

This was a very small group of people probably less than one hundred. Their life provided them with absolute luxury. I had one personal experience concerning their lifestyle. After my business was nationalized, I went back to my profession as a mechanical engineer, mostly working for structural steel companies running production. In my first job, the company manufactured all the steel production for a highly regarded communist effort: a hundred thousand people capacity sports stadium. When I got there the project was a year behind from finishing. We provided steel components like doors, light posts, railing, fences, etc. I don't remember what the problem was but they asked me to come to the stadium. I was scared of the meeting which solved all kinds of technical problems. There was one about our product, so after the meeting they took me to the source of the problem that I agreed to correct by sending people from the shop.

Since this was the first time I had been on location, they showed me around. We were close to the main viewing area for the top communist rulers. They showed me a tunnel which led to an underground garage. They told me the viewing area where the marble floor could be heated was built for forty people. The garage was for 120 cars because each person arrived with three identical cars. Nobody knew which car the big shot was sitting. Behind the seating area was a large buffet and a salon next to it. I was told the tunnels were one mile long with a large entry area to house with substantial security force.

They had their own stores from grocery to shoe. They have the best of everything. They had the first credit cards not because they paid for everything but for the store employees to think so.

Their homes were confined in one area, and then the area was fenced and guarded. Their vacation homes, on the shores of Lake Balaton, were also a guarded area.

They were completely isolated and guarded from the public and seldom visible. They never wrote about their private life, families, health, successes, etc. They were never seen in public with Russian high command stationed in Budapest area. They never went on foreign trips and hardly ever visited with Communist leadership in neighboring countries.

A large group of the top Echelon originated from the short-lived and ill-fated 1919 Hungarian Communist Revolution. This group was nurtured in Moscow by the Stalin government up to the time of the Russian occupation of Hungary and transplanted to west Hungary practically following the Russian army.

The first cabinet already had a few Communist members. They paved the way to a communist dictatorship in only three years. The transfer of power was accomplished through rigged elections and relentless witch hunt of the democratically elected politicians based on carefully orchestrated details from Moscow with the emphasis to avoid any accusation from any Russian involvement in the process.

The joint stupidity of the Western powers to trust Stalin after WWII with the free development of half of Europe created the modern-day slavery of more than a hundred million people for more than a quarter century.

Millions ended up in concentration camps, received substandard medical care, tortured, killed, lived under borderline standard of living etc.

The ruling class' education, former accomplishments, marital status or family were unknown. Nobody knows if they ever had hobbies or enjoyed any sport. Nobody had religion. It was a godless barbaric bunch.

One day, even the most trusted member could became a traitor, and would be executed for the most horrible crimes. Then he or she was never heard about again.

The passenger compartment of every car that they used was curtained off on four sides. The news hardly showed them arriving or exiting from a place. They were just there and never were surrounded by secret police.

They only smiled when small girls greeted them with flowers. They never walked up or down the stairs or even to and from airplanes.

I never spoke to anybody who ever met anybody or was close to anybody. It was a scary bunch.

The "Underground"

The underground was mostly an unorganized group of people, real and imaginary. Real ones were never discovered, the others never existed. It was the communist's tool to eliminate uninvolved elements in the communist leadership or groups of Hungarians considered dangerous for the communist order.

The most widespread group was millions of Hungarians who hated the Communists and grabbed any means to sabotage the government. They were not organized nor followed specific goals as they were mere individuals who caused ruin, destruction, the slowing down any purpose, etc.—making sure the government could not identify the perpetrators.

The most common was stealing. They steal anything that wasn't nailed down. The most efficient people were those who worked in warehouses. The variety was endless. The only criterion was it could fit in an individual's pocket. In a steel factory where I was working, screw and nuts, welding rods, steel brushes, gloves, aprons, and so on were stolen. People mostly never had any use for the stuff they stole.

In public buildings, factories, and office buildings, they stole light bulbs, ruined faucets, and broken windows. In many restaurants, they stole anything from silverwares to cups to glasses. One time, I visited a large manufacturing company with a large lunchroom, the only silverwares were soup spoons with holes drilled into it because the good ones were stolen.

The other items stolen were clothing, food, wine, liquor, soap, and shampoo from hotels. The list was endless.

To start at the top, the best-known underground objective was the political conspiracy to kill the political leaders or to create major sabotage etc. The whole conspiracy was dreamt up by the top members of government to eliminate notable communists. The whole crime was a three-ring circus for weeks with the main character sentenced to death.

The variation to the above process was when the important figure was simply eliminated, disappeared from public view one day from another. All of the fallen victims died of an accident or a heart attack.

The common underground conspiracy was committed by former members of the military or past second line political figures. They were sent to jail or to labor camps or killed during the investigation.

I, myself, was never aware of any political or other conspiracy except in three occasions. The first one was in late 1948 when a friend of mine asked to meet him on a popular street corner in Budapest. He told me that he was asked to find a place for an American somebody for two to three nights in the following week. I promised him I would try to find one but I was unsure that I could help him. Before we parted I told him to give me two days to try connecting. I sure didn't have any idea what to do. I could use the telephone and ask friends around lest I endanger anybody or myself that I undertook this project.

Then I had a great idea. The priest at my former high school was still teaching and he lived in a fenced compound with more than a hundred people. My class master, I thought, would have no problem hiding him. I went out to visit him but he denied help. Years later, I discovered that he was a communist lover but he never caused harm because of my questionable request from him. I called my friend telling him that I couldn't help him.

The second one was much later, probably early fifties. I was asked by my uncle's friend to visually inventory the Russian military plans at close at the military airport. He heard from my uncle that the company I was working for had fabricated and installed steel doors for the Russian military hangars. It was a difficult undertaking because I could only accomplish it at night because during the day I was working. The problem was I had to dream up some story where I was going at night. I had accomplished the task.

The third episode was a spooky one. My former tennis coach who finished the Air Force academy had kept in touch and visited me in the 1950's. He asked me to help him with a simple task. I was supposed to be in Budapest the following Sunday in a certain place—alone at 11:00 a.m. A middle-aged male was going to approach me (apparently he had my description) and ask me what time it was. I had to tell him it was 10:30 (regardless of the existing time). I went to the location on the specific day and time. The guy showed up, I told him the time, and the whole thing was finished.

The Communist Life

There was no private business. Everybody worked for the state. The exception were doctors, artists, lawyer, cooperatives, etc. After the companies, large or small, were nationalized, they were run by three people: the president, the secretary of the Communist Party, and the secretary of the union. Some of the presidents had high school education, most had only eight years of primary school. The presidents grew up in the ranks of the party. They had to finish the "Red Academy" which was a higher level of communist indoctrination mixed with some basic math, reading, writing, etc. The Communist Party was secretly the head of the workplace. Their most important job was weekly meetings which everyone had to attend—a nonstop praising of the Communist Party. The secretary had to be a longtime member of the party, from a family of a blue-collar worker, no background or ever owned a business or involved with any capitalist organization or part of a military or government association. Jewish background was a passport to a higher office since they were for sure clear of Nazi opposition.

Every law was strictly enforced. There was no critic of any rule. If it was publicly voiced, it was a sure entry to a labor camp.

The poverty was unbroken and extending to everybody except leaders of the party, company presidents, artists, leading sport figures, etc. We, my wife and I, had good jobs. I was an engineer with a lower management status. My wife was a grade school teacher and we could spend both of our salaries for food for the four of us in a week or for a pair of shoes. A winter coat was a major expense.

The communist rule was all-encompassing. Because of my background, our kids were lucky if they could finish high school. I probably could have improved my life if I had the stomach to join the party and catering to people who were way below my intellectual level.

The living conditions were, to some people, unbearable. We were lucky because we lived with my wife's parents. They were also lucky because if we didn't live with them, the local government could move in to their house a family with kids. In Budapest, many apartment houses were bombed out, collapsed, or unsafe to be occupied so the city couldn't house the original population. On top of that, thousands and thousands of apartments were taken over by a new communist middle class. Thus the available apartments were occupied by two to three families, each family occupying one room and a joint kitchen and bathroom. In this condition, each family had a certain time when they could use the kitchen and bathroom. They divided the expenses of the facility. Because of the conditions, there were no divorces, complicated marriages, and a generally complicated private life.

The Border

After ending military confrontation in Europe, the borders were opened, not intentionally but by uncertain responsibility of the individual state's military and settling down of the occupational military. Also, there was a large group of people who escaped to the West to avoid the Russians. Some of this displaced population never returned home and others had been gradually forced to return because of financial realities. The Hungarian border guards first checked border crossing traffic then extended their control over the terrain.

The critical border was that of Austria since that was the only noncommunist state that has a border with Hungary. A hundred-yard strip next to the Austrian border was plowed clean—with trees and bushes removed and installed with invisible field mines. There were hundreds of watchtowers with powerful searchlights erected in visible distance from each other and manned 24/7 by guards with shoot to kill orders to make certain that unhappy Hungarians are staying put. The communists established a thirty to forty mile strip by the Austrian border where everybody needed a permit to enter. Even these preparations could not stop people from escaping from Hungary. Many paid with their lives trying to pass the minefield. Before the Revolution of 1956 giving in to the Austrian government complains that Austrian people living on the border were injured by the exploding land mines. They removed all the land mines. This made it possible during the Hungarian Revolution in 1956 for two hundred thousand Hungarians to escape to the West—my family included.

Our First Attempt

There was no doubt about it in my mind when I laid eyes on the first Russian soldier back in 1945. There is only one way to provide a normal life—get out of the country. I was out of the country during my smuggling time but I just got married and my wife became pregnant, so I had to postpone my trip for two to three years, never thinking about whether Russia would close the border or that it was impossible to escape. But all of a sudden, in 1956, they picked up the mines. The watchtowers and the roaming border guards remained in place and there is also the permit requirement.

I don't know how many escape plans I dreamt up. But after close look, they were all too risky. But one of them became more and more possible. I was always involved with fishing and I know lots of fishermen. There were numerous small rivers and a large lake in the border zone. I could develop a long weekend fishing vacation for the whole family, get border permits, rent a bus, overwhelm the driver, and drive across the border. Once we were in the border zone, we could go back and forth to look for the best fishing spots and find a location that was best to cross the border (it couldn't be a road because they were all controlled). I thought I could organize the whole thing in two months. I had to select very carefully eight to ten families who were willing to take the risk. The biggest selling point was that if we couldn't find a safe location to jump the border, we just had to have a good time and cancel out the whole adventure. The presence of the wives and children made the whole plan not suspicious. I found the bus company and finalized attendance.

Everybody applied for the border pass. Everybody received one except me and my family. There was no way for the group to go without me because if the group was successful, I would end up in jail for a long time.

Revolution

On October 23, 1956, my wife and I had dinner with our good friends, Feri and Klari at their home on Castle Hill in Buda. Feri and Klari were older than we were. They met in San Paulo, Brazil, where Klari was a teacher in a Hungarian elementary school and Feri was working for his uncle who was consul for Hungary. They got married in Brazil and transferred back to Hungary after WWII broke out.

I knew the whole family, and I was always interested in Feri's and Klari's stories when they lived in Brazil. After dinner, we went home early because all four of us had to go to work the next day. We went home with a city bus which passed the radio building on its route home. To our big surprise, the driver announced that he would avoid passing the radio building because there was a large crowd closing off the street. At home, we turned on the radio. It was speaking about some political meeting that was scheduled for the next day. Not a word about the large group of people by the radio building.

In the morning, there was a sound of small arms firing in the distance. The sound was practically uninterrupted. There was no public transportation in the city. The revolution encompassed the whole city. Tens of thousands of Russian troops with tanks entered the city. They and the police took down the demonstrators. The radio was taken over by the revolutionists. The Hungarian army gave arms to the rebels.

The seeds of the revolution started in 1944 when the first Hungarian woman was raped by a Russian soldier. That was twelve years ago. Rape and looting were crimes of individual Russian soldiers which were tolerated by the invading Russian command. Deportation of Hungarians to Russian labor camps were ordered by the Kremlin. The Hungarians expressed their rage as soon as they could in the 1945 election. In the past, the Communist Party was illegal. Now the exiled communist Hungarians (exiled after WW I) came home with Russian troops. Trained in totalitarian techniques, they were certain in election victory but they received only 17% of the votes. With the Russian presence on their side, they were included in a coalition government of all parties. The communist took charge of all the important ministry of the interior, which included the already red-infiltrated security police.

The Communists pursued their prime objective of breaking the majority of the Smallholders Party. Slowly they marginalized the leaders of the party then jailed them, etc.

The final elimination of the organized opposition went on. The social democrats were forced to merge with the Communists. Other opposition parties were dissolved. The power of any communist resistance, the Catholic Church, was breached by persecutions which culminated in the treason trial and imprisonment of Joseph Cardinal Mindszenty. By May 1949, the Russian-style election finally gave the unopposed Communist Party the kind of majority they expected from a satellite which is 95% of the vote.

The head of the Communists who took over was a lifelong follower of the party's most radical practice. His name was Rakosi. He handed the Hungarian economy to Moscow, not only as extension of the Russian economy but also to serve as experimentation of the new policies. The major goal was to industrialize the once rich agricultural economy.

When Stalin died in 1953 Rakosi left his power. He worked for a more consumer-oriented communist who returned Rakosi's job after a short time. When Khrushchev came to power, he tried de-Stalinization, and Rakosi fell again. The new press gave voice for criticism of the communists. People who were jailed during the Rakosi-era were freed. Both the Russians and the Hungarians were aware of the hatred the Hungarians had against the communist order but hoped the continued reconciliation of operations would be enough to cool the tension. But Hungary was beyond reconciliation. It exploded to full-scale revolution.

The first two days' actions were so overwhelming that the rebels demanded the Russians to leave. On the third day, the fighting slowed down and both sides dig in.

If the next couple of days didn't promise victory, I would leave the country regardless of the danger of being captured. All the alternatives were discussed: I am going alone; Maria and I would go; we only take Tibor because he is ten years old and represents less danger than Steve who was only two. The border was less than one hundred and fifty miles away. A bicycle came up in the discussion but was cancelled out because it was only practical if Maria and I went and it was unknown what control on the road the Russians or Communists would initiate. The firm decision was all four of us would go and we would take the train as close to the border as possible and go on foot to the border.

On the fourth day, twenty-six of October, the revolution extended to the province. In Budapest, it was "relatively" calm. This was the first day I left home and walked close to two hours to find out what was going on in the former central office of the Smallholders Party. It was occupied by a large group of people on the outside. I knew many people from the 1945 election and I had my membership identification with me so the guard at the door let me in. The inside was also occupied. I poked my way around asking everybody what was going on. They said that they were looking for people who were familiar with the Russian's position. I told a guard by the door that I just walked from the suburbs. They let me in. In the room there were around twenty people in groups of three to four. I looked around, I didn't know a soul. Most of them were much older than me. One man asked me to come over to their table. They asked me about

Russian positions on my way into the city. I only saw dead Russians in military cars, lots of burned out Russian cars and trucks but no active military on my whole trip. I remained in the room telling them the location of several police garages and Russian storehouses I knew about. My information dated back to my smuggling days and they were outdated. From that day on, every day I went back and forth from the suburb to the downtown.

On the days of October 26th to 30th included local skirmishes mostly with rebel soldiers. Hungarian and Russian negotiations concerning the withdrawal of Russian troops from Budapest had started. In the meantime, the Russian military had brought in reinforcements from the neighboring satellite countries. A high-ranking Hungarian military group was invited to the Russian headquarters south of the city including General Maleter, the new defense minister, for a negotiation. When they arrived, they were guided to a waiting room. All of them were killed minutes after arrival. Cardinal Mindszenty took refuge in the United States embassy. On the second of November, Russian tanks sealed the Hungarian-Austrian border. On the fourth of November, hundreds of Russian tanks occupied Budapest. The Russian troops looted the city. From the eleventh of November, the Russian conducted mass deportation of Hungarians to Russian slave labor camps. I am still going back and forth to the city. A General strike started and collapsed. By the seventeenth of November, the last resistance in the city was eliminated.

That night, I went home deciding I'm not going back to the city again. The same night, a friend of the family came over to visit us and told me I better do something because the next day I was going to be arrested. Maria and I decided we were going to leave the next morning. We were mentally prepared and already organized what we were going to take with us. Identification, birth certificates, my driver's license, three sets of underwear, loaf of bread, a chunk of boneless shoulder ham, a bottle of rum, and clothes that we had on. That was it.

Next morning, we waited for Maria's parents to leave home for work and then we left without anybody knowing.

Freedom

It was final. The Russian military killed the revolution. The biggest problem was that we didn't know what the conditions on the border were. We heard of people leaving for the border.

We needed a sleeping pill for Steve. We could not gamble on him crying for any reason on the border. Maria ran over to Steve's doctor who lived close by to pick up some sleeping pills. It was a cold winter but there was no snow on the ground. We all had heavy coats and winter shoes. Tibor had an old fur coat that we took for Steve to sleep in. We also brought cloth diapers. No change of clothing for anybody. Next morning, when Maria's parents left, we left also with all the money we had in a leather case. Nothing for the kids.

We walked out of the house and looked back thinking, are we never going to see the house again (as I am writing this book fifty years later, we never went back and never saw the house again)? The morning was cold and cloudy as we were walking toward the train terminal for trains going south or southwest. As we were walking, while Maria carried Steve, a truck came up from behind us. Maria tried to stop the truck, it stopped and the driver asked where we were going. We said to the train station (a long distance from us not having public transportation). He said he will take us over there. We asked how much it will cost, he said nothing. When we departed he wished us good luck. He knew where we were going.

The train station was not very busy. Would any train go toward the direction of the Austrian border? I bought three tickets while Steve was going free. As I was leaving the ticket counter, there was a couple with a boy of Tibor's age coming by. The father was my classmate in high school. We hadn't seen each other since graduation. They were trying to escape also from the country. His wife's name was Juci, my schoolmate's Laci, and their son's Lacika. After they bought the ticket, we joined with Maria and the kids. All of us were happy that we ran into each other. It gave us a sense of security and the fact that we were not alone.

As we walked toward the train, Maria's girl friend who lived in our neighborhood came toward us with a young guy who is probably of high school age. We found out that the guy was her nephew who also intended to go. She was working at the train station serving food in normal times. She asked if her nephew could join us. We said okay. She offered to find what route the train will go off to and when it was supposed to reach its destination. When she came back, she informed us that we would leave in two hours, going south then turning west to reach the border on late afternoon of the following day.

The train was not going to travel during the night because there was a rumor that Russian planes were shooting the trains going in a western direction. There were eight of us, so we occupied a cabin with wood benches a third class accommodation. Nobody had luggage, just a bag or rucksack. That meant that we could use the overhead shelves for sleeping if necessary. We were worried that they were going to empty the train for the night. We left the train station at 1:00 p.m. The train was going from slow to medium speed because it was an unscheduled run, we thought. The afternoon went by fast, we were getting familiar with each other again. We exchanged stories. Laci's family had a good-sized factory making ladders for general use and for fire departments. They were nationalized the same day as mine. Juci was a seamstress who made custom dresses for well-to-do customers. Paul who just joined us, just graduated from high school and intended to go to France to join his relatives on his father's side.

When the train finally stopped, it was already dark. We were told we should not worry about Russian planes because they never attacked in a train station. Many people got out of the train. Everybody was going west mostly without final destination. They were mostly young people, young married couples and very few people with children. The train station was empty and the lights were turned off. There was no service of any kind but fresh water. The girls ended up sleeping with the kids, Maria was with Steve while Laci and me were in sitting position, and Paul and Tibor on the overhead shelf.

The evening went by without any problem. The only sound was from dogs barking in the distance and the repetitive hissing of the steam engine. The cabin was comfortably warm. From time to time the conductor passed our cabin with a flashlight sweeping the cabin. Outside was dark with heavy clouds covering the sky.

We woke up early to the shaking of the wagon and the speeding up staccato of the wheels. We passed by Lake Balaton as the train turned west towards the border. The ride was a continuous stop and go. We stopped more than two hours in one place. We gave money to the conductor, the mechanist and the helper because they knew how to help people escape. The conductor continuously kept us up to date as to where we were and how long we have to go. It became dark and we were still going when all of a sudden the train stopped and let everybody who is escaping, leave. It was 9 o'clock. The moon was out and only hidden from time to time behind thin clouds. The visibility was quite good. By the time we got off and got organized, there wasn't a soul around from the train. The track was two to three feet elevated. We were on the edge of a grassy area with small bushes close and in the distance. The place was flat, not a building in any place. The train slowly disappeared.

We started to walk in one line, one behind the other when we discovered that Paul disappeared. We were not surprised, the kid's an added risk. He hardly ever spoke to us, so good luck to him. Maria was carrying Steve who was sleeping. Juci was the most concerned in the group, she warned us if we were speaking loud. The boys, Tibor and Lacika, were very alert telling us what they could see. We all walked very slowly, Maria was in front while I was right behind her ready to catch her if she would fall because her vision was very distracted carrying Steve.

We walked on a very visible dirt path when all of a sudden both Laci and I discovered that we had no idea what direction we were going. My association with the outdoors was limited and went back to my Boy Scout years. We were walking perpendicular to the train track assuming that the train was going parallel with the border to reach its final destination. Then Laci and I remembered the old rule that mosses would grow only on the north side of the tree. The whole area was full of small bushes but no trees. All of us saw that there was a group of trees in the distance. When we got there, I had to climb halfway up the trees to find moss. We were going the wrong direction. We were going northwest instead of west. We changed directions until there was no more path. We had to walk on a pretty rough terrain until there were no more bushes but instead small stones and grass.

We decided to sit down on the edge of a large boulder because we were walking for two hours nonstop. When we stood up, we continued going now in the right direction and we ended up on a path. As we were walking, the moon was blocked by a large, black cloud. When it became bright again we were walking on the edge of a deep mine of some kind that created a large, deep ditch. There was enough light to see how deep it was. In the distance was a house with some lights on and a dog barking, the sound breaking up in the distance. As we were discussing how to try to reach the house Tibor discovered other house roofs shining in the dark. This house was way south from the lit up one but closer to us. We decided to try to reach that house.

As we went closer, the house was dark. It was sitting next to a train line with the gate pointing up. We reached the door and knocked on it. Somebody turned on the light. A middle-aged man opened the door and saw Maria with Steve in her arms. He asked us to come inside. It was nice and warm. His wife came out to the room which was a kitchen. We introduced ourselves and told them we intended to go over to Austria and ask them if we can stay in the house until the next evening. They were both very accommodating. She gave us butter and bread. We took out our leftover ham. The Laci's had salami while she made tea. Everybody was hungry. We told them our story. They told us we were more than fifteen kilometers from the border etc. They also told us that there is a young couple from Budapest sleeping in a room. They arrived hours ago. They said we can only sleep on the kitchen floor. They put some heavy sacks on the floor. I had a fur lined coat which was large enough to cover Maria and me and Tibor between us. She took the sleeping Steve put him in the crib with her sleeping son. It was 3:00 a.m. when we turned the lights off.

Steve woke us up. The young couple was in uniform. They were working at Budapest's public transportation. He was driving a bus while she was a conductor. They told us the Russians are moving from the north to the south and that they closed the border. They asked if we saw the sky lit up with flares shot by the Russians. We said no. They said that early in the evening when they arrived here, they could see many flares in a far distance. He said apparently the Russians are not far away from us. Our hosts said the house north from here (the house we saw lit up with the dog barking) had Russian soldiers.

We told the hosts we would like to hire some locals who were familiar with the area to guide us to the border. He said he had relatives in the town close by and later in the day, he would go into town and locate somebody. Our lady host fixed all of us breakfast and lunch. She gave Maria diapers.

The male host went into town after lunch, when he came back, he said he found two young guys who will show up before dark and guide us to the border. The young couple said they will go on their own. We gave money to the host (he objected to it but the wife took it). The afternoon went by in no time. When the two kids arrived on bicycles, we gave them money that they asked for. We waited an hour after the sun went down, gave Steve sleeping pills, said goodbye, and left.

We were not gone for more than half an hour when we started seeing flares, but they were not very far, probably ten kilometers away. The kids went in the front, we were behind them. The visibility was pretty bad. As we were walking, they always pointed in the direction of the border. Juci was holding onto one kid's bicycle. When we reached a wooded area, the kids told us we should stay put because they want to go forward to look for a path. They left and never came back. I took over carrying Steve. He was bundled up in Tibor's fur coat. He was facing me while I was holding onto him. He was always falling back and I had to catch him, so I held the neck of the coat in my mouth, and it was working. As I was walking in the front, three guys jumped out from a bush, holding flashlights in our faces. The guy who didn't have a rifle came to me asking what was in the package I was carrying. When I showed him Steve, he jumped back saying, "oh my God." They were Hungarian border guards. The guy who spoke to me was the leader. He was a gypsy. He told the other two to turn off the flashlight. We told them we were looking for the Austrian border. I reached in my pocket and gave him all my leftover Hungarian money, so did Laci. I watched Laci and Steve, they were laying in the ground face down. The gypsy told them, "Don't worry, stand up." Maria pulled her ring off of her finger and gave it to him. We were clear of trees before us. He told the other two to show us the bridge and he pointed on a light in the distance telling us that the light is in Austria. He stayed while the two soldiers walked behind us and guided us to a narrow wood bridge. One of the soldiers told us to go straight to the direction of the light then they went back. Feeling safe, we started talking loud when people around us hiding in the bushes warned us to keep silent. We said we are in Austria. At least thirty people stood up arguing with each other and us. Walking a short distance, we could see one Austrian border guard waving the light back and forth. When we went closer, there was a small, one-room border station. When they discovered Steve in my arms, they asked us to come in. I told them that he was drugged and we need medical help. They took Steve and we left the room, waiting for the doctor. The soldiers were massaging his legs, and by the time the doctor arrived, Steve was sitting up eating a banana. The doctor gave him orange juice, checked him out and told us he was okay.

November 21

The border town was Mosendorf. It was 10:00 p.m. when they took us with a bus to a close by town further in from the border. Maria, Juci, and the kids went to sleep in a farmhouse and Laci and I ended up in the gym of a local school. The gym floors on both sides were filled with straw. There were already people there who arrived earlier.

Maria and Juci and the kids had a chance to get washed. This was when Magda discovered, after taking Tibor's boots off, that his right foot was full of blood. The boots were giving him blisters and he never complained a word about it. The ladies of the farmhouse gave Magda clean socks and ointment to put on his feet.

November 22, 23

For two days, we stayed in the border town. During the day, we walked around in the small town. We were fed in the gym. I spoke to locals who were all surprised about the condition in Hungary. They were aware that there was dictatorship and bad conditions, but they were horrified to discover the details of our lives over there.

The second night before falling asleep, I had a chance to reflect on what happened. The details of the escape and the new life did not leave too much time to realize the unbelievable change we provided for us and the kids. Here we were in a foreign world, not knowing where we were going to be tomorrow, where we were going to end up and when. Still, we feel absolutely secure. No more tyranny, hopeless future for ourselves and the kids, permanent poverty, and so on. The new life was going to be freedom, looking forward to the future and unrestricted education for our boys. We turned to God for hope and some in our determination to carry out a better life.

November 26

The next day, we went to Jennersdorf, then by bus and train to Klagenfurt arriving there on twenty-sixth of November, 1956. It was a gorgeous ride. There was a stream going along the railroad and snowy mountains all around us. We could hear a cowbell ringing when the trains stopped. We all felt we were living in a dream. It was 6:00 p.m. when we boarded a bus at the train station which took us to the (Ursulinen) school in town.

It was a large, one-story building with a large courtyard. We were welcomed by a group of nuns, some of them spoke Hungarian. Maria's aunts were both well-known in Klagenfurt so we were privileged to receive a private room. The nuns rolled in an extra bed because there can be only six people in the room. We met two other couples from the train. I asked the nuns if they had another private room because they were good friends. They also gave them a private room next to us.

Next day, officials from the city took us to a used clothes warehouse where we were able to pick up two sets of clothes, underwear, coats, etc. It took us all morning until we found the right clothing for the four of us. We kept our shoes and overcoat. Once we got back to the cloister, we took a shower, changed into the new clothing, ditched the old one, and felt like a million dollars.

In the afternoon we went to the register with the new organization that was responsible to take us to the United States. From there, we went to the place where we registered for our Austrian papers. After the police discovered that I spoke fluent German, they offered me a job as a translator to work six days of the week with good pay.

November 27

After we went home and had dinner in the cloister's dining room, we decided to go out and look around in the neighborhood. We were told to be back by 8:00 p.m. when they closed the doors. There were many Austrians waiting outside. They offered us cookies and money and wanted to talk to us. There was a Hungarian couple where the man owned a knitting shop. When Maria told him that she was working in Hungary with knitting machines, he offered her a job that Maria took.

Laci and Juci could not believe that on our first day in Klagenfurt we already both had a job. We put the kids to bed and sat down with Juci and Laci—the first no rush evening we had since we left Hungary. Our neighbors just also got home, so the eight of us had a lot to talk about. The younger couple, Mara and Paul, was our age. They had a six-year-old daughter. We were mostly together with them. The older couple had a son. They pretty much stayed to themselves. I don't remember their names. Both couples intended to go to California. Our old friend Laci and Juci had to go to Canada because their good friends left Budapest after WWII and they were partners in Laci's business.

November 28

The next night, we decided to go back to the city and do some window shopping. Generally, we included Juci and Laci. As we went out from the cloister, we met a couple named Susie and Dithelm. They were locals. Dithelm owned a drugstore that was strictly involved with medication. From this point on, we were together with them daily. Dithelm spent two years in the United States as a prisoner of war during WWII. He was in a camp in Texas. On this first night with them we went downtown, it was like a Christmas picture book. Snow was all over. Every light post was decorated with ornaments and Christmas lights. The lampposts were connected above the street with decorations and lights. Every store was reflecting Christmas spirit. It was beautiful. The show windows had merchandise on display—what we hadn't seen in ten years—not just the quality but the volume of gifts. Dithelm showed their pharmacy and introduced us to his sister who was working there. We sat down in a sweet shop that hardly existed in Budapest. The kids had never seen sweet products and were very content with the first bite. We went home eating too much, enjoying the luxury of a free society.

November 29

On the next day, while working in the police station, an Austrian middle-aged man started conversation with me. He was interested in what was going on in Hungary, what was my profession, etc. Before he left, he gave me his name card and told me he liked to speak to me more because he would be interested in hiring me. He had a large machine shop on the edge of town. I would call him and he would pick me up and show me the place.

Later that day, a lady came to the police station. When she saw me, she came over to me telling me that she was the one who registered us to the NCWC. She told me that the NCWC is a Catholic organization, and since most Hungarians are Catholic, we were going to be in Austria a long time before they reach us. Her suggestion was that we switch over to the Tolstoy Foundation (which was part of Rockefeller Foundation)—which only had permission to handle 1200 people—so that our chance of going to the United States would be faster. Before I left the police station that day, I asked my boss to be late the next morning because of the opportunity with the Tolstoy Foundation.

At night around 5:00 p.m., Dithelm showed up and said that is taking us to his home for dinner. His sister was there with her fiancé. His son was out of town as he was an Olympic horseman and always on the road. The dinner was excellent but hard for me because I was the only one who spoke German. Maria started to catch up but needed some time. I told them my story with the Tolstoy Foundation and my run-in with the owner of the machine shop. Dithelm, who spent time in the United States, was empathically against us staying in Austria. In his opinion, the potential for us was unbelievably better in the United States than here. I agreed with him but told him I would just go and see his shop because I was interested in new machinery. In Hungary, the newest equipment that I got used to dated back in the mid-thirties. We got home before 8 o'clock, put the kids to bed, got together with our Hungarian neighbors, and told stories.

November 30

Next morning after breakfast, we all went over to the Tolstoy Foundation to register. We told them that we already registered with NCWC. They said they will call them. As we were walking home, Laci pulled me aside and told me that they were embarrassed that we are working and going to get paid. He said he had with him an old gold watch that he would like to sell and I should go with him to a jeweler because he can't speak German. Juci took the kids back home, Laci picked up the watch, and Maria went to the knitting shop. Laci and I went looking for a jewelry shop and we found one downtown. We went into the store and I asked for the owner. He was a white and bearded older guy. I told him the story of the watch and introduced Laci who is the third generation owner of the watch and wanted to sell it. He took a large magnifying glass on his head and opened the lid of the watch and then the back, examining every detail. Then he said the watch is not gold, but because it is very old he is interested in buying it, offering $150. If the watch had been gold, he would probably offer within $250. Laci was really shocked but accepted the $150. When we left, he told me that he was hoping to sell the watch for one hundred dollars. He was wondering if somebody cheated his grandfather because it was considered a family treasure.

December 1

It was Friday, both Maria and I got paid. With money in our pockets, we asked Laci and Juci to come shopping with us. We went to the sweet shop and picked up some delicacies then a medium-sized luggage. But the most important was a small bottle of Coca-Cola. When we got home, we all tasted it and liked it. If you lived under communist rule, Coke was a forbidden drink. You were supposed to get all kinds of sickness from it. We had a good dinner then went out for a walk. After the kids went to bed, like every night, we got together with the neighbors. It was a lively conversation every night. One of the subjects was what will happen to us when we leave Europe and where were we going to end up. Mara asked Maria if she ever did séance. We discovered that with the exception of Juci, all three ladies did.

The Quija board is a popular fortune-telling tool. It is a fourteen-inch by fourteen-inch white cardboard with a large circle. The ring is divided into squares, each square holding one letter of the English alphabet plus the numbers zero to nine. In the center of the board were two squares with the words yes, or no. The only other item that is needed is a silver coin which is over an inch in diameter. The participants (three or four people) sit around a small table with the cardboard in the center. They put the silver coin in the board and touching the coin with one finger, a participant asks for a dead person to be present. The dead person can be anybody, a relative, a famous person, or somebody who died yesterday or a thousand years ago. If the soul becomes present, the silver coin will move from one letter to the next with the answer. One person had to write down the sequence of the letters where the coin has moved. The hope is that the sequence of the letters depicts an answer. The participants who touch the coin were not moving the coin, they only follow the coin as it was moving.

December 2

On the next day after work, I picked up a piece of white cardboard and an unknown silver coin in a gift shop. Arriving home, I constructed the Quija board for the evening. By 8 o'clock all activity stopped. The kids were in bed and all eight of us were ready to look into the future. I myself had limited experience with the Quija board. It dated back to a couple of nights right before I was drafted into the service. I was working for the first time after college when one of my new colleagues and his girlfriend suggested the Quija board. Everybody agreed. It was interesting, but I walked away from it as a nonbeliever. The same group came together two weeks later and some of the answers we got had to be looked for in books and one of them on the world map. All the answers were correct and that left me thinking.

Maria had two interesting stories. Both of them dated back to her college-teaching years. It happened in the fourth year four to five months after the Russians occupied Budapest. It started months earlier when the Germans invaded the city. It was May 1944. The American bombing was nonstop and practically every day. The college was run by nuns who decided to close the school. After they opened up to finish the fourth year, there was no transportation in the city.

For Maria, who lived in the suburbs, it would take two hours in the morning and two hours in the afternoon to walk back and forth from the school. But she wasn't walking because she had an aunt who was an Ursulinen nun who was a director of a dormitory. She loved her aunt. Over the weekend, she walked home under the security of an old-time friend and same thing Monday on morning. The Russians never bothered anybody who had a male companion.

The girls in the dormitory were a lively bunch who many times played with the Quija board. All the girls were medical students. When exam time was coming, Maria was worried about physics. Her favored soul was Dante, a thirteenth century poet. He told Maria to study free fall. She told this to her best friend Margo. When the day of the examination came, all the girls who were tested were sitting in front with their back to the rest of the class. The nun teaching the subject handed each girl the subject they had to study. Maria drew magnetism. They received three minutes to think over their answers. Maria was beat, as she hardly knew anything about magnetism, but she thought she could come up with some answer. When the nun reached her, she asked if she was prepared to speak about magnetism. Maria replied yes. Then the Nun said OK then start talking about free fall. She was excellent. When the exam was over, her friend Margo said that Maria gave mental suggestion to the nun.

The week after was a piano exam. Margo was a real klutz in the piano. Margo suggested to Maria to ask the Quija board, and if it would give the right answer, she would believe in it. Her requirement was that Maria's friend write down the answer, bring it to school and give it to Margo the day before the exam, and that Maria should stay home the next day. Everything went according to her request. The Quija's suggestion was that she should get the H scale. Margo followed the advice. On the day before the test she practiced the H scale. Next day, when she was asked to play the piano, she got told to play the H scale. She fainted.

The second story happened on the last day of school. They asked Dante again. Instead, a Hungarian soldier came in. He spelled his name, age, and rank. He also told about his story when he was living in the suburb of Budapest where his grave was which is on the side of a creek. There was a wooden cross by his grave. On the cross was his helmet, and under the lining of the helmet was a letter to his fiancé with her address. He asked them to take the letter to her. The next day, a bunch of girls met where the grave was. When they located the grave one of the girls tried to take out the letter. She had a hard time because she was shaking so badly. Maria said that after that, and for years, she didn't touch the Quija board.

Back to the first evening, we tried out the board. The three girls sit around a table. The rest of us were sitting on the edge of our beds. I was the one who recorded the sequence of the letters and writing them in my notebook. Maria suggested calling Dante because in the past she had luck with him. Dante came in with no problem. Everybody was interested on how their relatives were. Everybody was okay except Maria's father who was in jail for two days after we left.

December 3

The days became routine. While Maria and I went to work, Laci and Juci babysit, the neighbors go sightseeing, Dithelm came over every day, etc. At night we have the Quija board. The answers were lately that, Maria, the kids, and I will leave Klagenfurt first, Laci and Juci the last ones. Also it was said that we were going to end up in the city of St. Joseph, Michigan and I will work for a retired Air Force Captain. We couldn't find an American map to see where St. Joseph was.

One day, Dithelm invited us after dinner to a nightclub. Both Juci and Laci had a really bad cold so they decided to stay. Dithelm picked us up. We went to a Shell gas station and in the basement was a bar. We ended up getting home at 11:00 p.m. We had to throw stones to our windows to wake up Laci and to let us in. He said that we got a call from the Tolstoy Foundation to be ready the next day at 7:00 a.m. because the bus was going to pick us up to go to Germany.

The next day, we woke up early to pack up and called Dithelm. We were on the bus when Dithelm arrived. We shook hands from the bus window. Dithelm was crying like a baby and so was Maria.

We were thirty to forty people on the bus, mostly families with kids. The bus took us to the train station. From there, we went to Salzburg by train. We arrived at Salzburg on December 11, 1956. It was Tuesday late in the evening. We stayed in Salzburg until the sixteenth of December in military barracks that the Americans used during the war.

On the first day, we had to go through a physical examination. The lines were long, but because we were registered with the Tolstoy Foundation, we went through the "back door." We were x-rayed, blood tested, and went through general physical examination. All four of us were in great shape. We got a clean bill of health. The same day, we visited the military store where we could shop using our gift money. We picked up underwear, socks, clothing, shoes for the boys, and also a second small luggage. After that, we were ready to go to Germany. The Russian objected to American military planes flying into Austria to pick up Hungarian refugees since Austria was a neutral country.

Every day, a bus took people from the camp to Salzburg to sightsee. We stayed in camp and while walking around the camp with the kids, the loudspeaker called our name. I went to the offices. A lady told us the bus would pick us up at 2:00 p.m. to go to Germany. We went back to the barracks and packed up our things. Actually, the bus left at 5:00 p.m. on December 16, 1956.

It was nine o'clock when our bus reached the German border. We had to stop for the border guards to inspect the bus. After the border guard walked through the bus, we were ready to cross into Germany. On the other side of the gate were two Jeeps and four motorcycles with soldiers sitting on them. They had the American flag on their uniform and a big sign which said MP. We had no idea what MP meant. The only thing we knew was that they were Americans. To actually see Americans waiting for us was such an incredible feeling of security and happiness. I wanted to cry and laugh. Finally we felt that we were out of the Communists' grip.

We were taken to an American military compound some place outside of Munich. A band played the American and Hungarian anthem as we got off the bus. We had dinner in the officer's mess hall and a big black soldier served us the dinner. Tibor got a drumstick. Tibor asked me what kind of bird it was. I said I had no idea and he should just eat it. We later found out, because it was close to Christmas, that it was a turkey. We had turkey in Hungary but not the size of that bird.

After dinner, we went into the army barracks where there was a line of bunk beds. We were told to find a place for ourselves, and when it was time to leave for the next stretch of the trip—this time to the United States—our names would be called. We sat on the bunks and wondered how long we would be staying there. The boys were pretty tired and sleepy after the big meal and the long bus ride, so we tried to make them comfortable.

No sooner had they stretched out that our names were called. We were the first ones called and were told to sit in the first row of chairs by the door. After all the people were called, we were told that our plane would be leaving at 11 o'clock that night for the United States. We had to leave the luggage and take our personal stuff and go out to a waiting bus. The bus took us to the airport and to a four-engine military plane. It was 11 o'clock when the plane started to taxi for the takeoff. The takeoff was bumpy, then smooth after it was airborne. Neither one of us had ever flown. It was a fabulous view when the plane turned and we could see Munich from the air.

The whole flight was a remarkable experience. The captain was Eisenhower's pilot. The copilot was a Korean veteran. The two stewardesses were all military members; and during the whole flight, never stopped helping the passengers. The captain spoke German. When he walked back and forth on the plane, he spent some time with us asking about our life behind the Iron Curtain. At one point he took Tibor to the cockpit. He was a great guy. We flew over London to our first stop in Ireland. We got off to stretch our legs and walked back and forth in the airport. Next was the flight over the ocean. We and the kids were sleeping most of the time during the flight over the ocean.

Everybody was bright-eyed when we got told by the captain that we were getting close to the shore. The next part of the flight was over lakes and forests covered with snow until we arrived to Gander, Newfoundland on the seventeenth of December at 3:30 p.m. We stayed close to the terminal. The plane was pretty fragrant from the disposed diapers. We had lots of kids on the plane. It was delightful to inhale some cold, fresh air. Red Cross ladies served us with tea that was black and thick as syrup, it tasted awful. We stayed there for a couple of hours.

When we were taxiing for takeoff, it was remarkable. The whole airfield was as shiny as an ice field. The next stop was New York. When we got there, it was an unbelievable sight. The city was lit up, a Christmas spectacle. We were flying for close to an hour above and around the city when the captain told us that we couldn't land because at lower elevations the air was full of pockets which would be rough for the kids, so he was going back to Boston.

After landing, we were greeted by the local Red Cross and the press. The press and photographer were with Hungarian travelers. I was so tired that I laid down on a wooden bench and fell asleep. We left Boston on bus, at 5:00 a.m., to Camp Kilmer in New Jersey, and arriving there at 5:30 p.m. The only remarkable thing was that as we go from one town to another there was nobody on the streets. During one of our stops on the road, we ran into an old Hungarian guy with a big, stinky cigar who told us we were lucky to have left Hungary and come here.

Camp Kilmer was a working military base. We were housed in one of the many one-story barracks. We had the corner section with four beds, two and two facing each other. On one side of the barracks was a room for a sergeant who was the boss of the barracks. On the other side, there were showers and toilets. The showers were available for men or women in certain times.

A short walk from the barracks was the mess hall. For every breakfast, lunch, or dinner, we lined up before a counter where military guys were serving food. The food was unbelievable in variety and volume. We sat behind long tables and in the center of the table there were all kinds of jams, butter, ketchup, etc. When the meal was finished, one soldier went around the tables and put in the garbage barrel any food from the center that was open. Somebody could take a small corner off with the tip of a knife, it went to the garbage. A good-sized jar full with apricot jam if opened went to the garbage. We could not believe it.

On the second day in Camp Kilmer, we were lining up for breakfast in the mess hall when we discovered a large US map on the wall. We rushed over to search for St. Joseph, Michigan. There it was on the shores of Lake Michigan practically across from Chicago. I was a duck in my previous life so living on the shores of a lake was paradise for me.

This was also the day we registered with the Tolstoy Foundation. They had a small office. We ended up with a middle-aged lady who spoke Hungarian. She looked us up in her paperwork. She read out loud the information she had. When she got to Maria, she asked Maria's maiden name that was in her paperwork and asked Maria again. Then she said, "Do you have a relative who was a military officer?" Maria said yes, her uncle. The lady screamed out, "I was engaged to him." They asked each other around, with a big story telling on both sides. She said finally, "I am going to get a good place for you."

On another day, we were lining up for lunch when behind us a middle-aged lady with kids, all teenagers, were telling jokes. Maria said she was going to turn around and check who they were (in Hungary, turning around to look at somebody was very impolite) then she said they were her aunt and her kids. And I said, "Yes, they are in Camp Kilmer and you have your aunt right behind us." Yes she was.

They lived far away from us in Hungary, closer to the Austrian border. She was a teacher and was divorced for a long time. The two girls and one boy were between sixteen to eighteen years of age. After this discovery, we were in touch with them all the time. From that moment on we spent many hours with them including all the meals.

Another day, our friends arrived. They were held back because both kids' x-rays showed suspicious detail. Repeated x-rays cleared them. When we met them in the camp, Mary asked who we were because during their registration at Tolstoy Foundation, they were handled very routinely up to the point they told them their friends are the Zaks. After that, they got the red carpet treatment.

Mary went to Teacher College with a girl who, after WWII, ended up in Germany with her father who was a police officer. She met an American soldier and they fell in love. The soldier was sent for a week to another part of Germany. During the week, Mary's father had a chance to get back to Hungary, so they packed up and left. When the American soldier returned, Mary was gone. Norman got back to the United States and the only thing he knew about Mary was her name and that she was living in Budapest. It took him a year to find Mary. He got Mary a visa. She came to the United States and they got married. Mary and Maria kept in touch all the time. Maria knew only Mary's maiden name and that she lived in New Jersey.

My high school schoolmate Pityu was four years older than me. He came to the United States after WWII and ended up in New York. He came over to Camp Kilmer every weekend looking for friends. When we ran into each other in Camp Kilmer, Magda asked Pityu if they could locate Mary by giving her name in Metuchen. He found her. Maria called Mary. Mary invited us over to spend the days around Christmas with them. We didn't even know that we could leave the camp. We went back to the lady at the Tolstoy Foundation who said that we could go. We packed our stuff for the visit and we left the next morning after Mary picked us up.

We arrived at Mary's home two days before Christmas. They had a large house. Her husband was in the business of making driveways from the street to the garage. They reorganized one room for four of us to sleep. The next morning, Maria bathed Steve and discovered that he had brownish and pink blemishes all over his face, back, and chest. Maria and Mary's physicians diagnosed measles. Mary's three children, a girl and two boys were aged four, eight and six respectively. Neither one of them had measles, but Mary wasn't concerned. She hoped they will all get it over with. Mary got in touch with the camp's doctor who came out and diagnosed measles. He said it should be over in ten days. We had to see him to check out before we can get back to the camp.

We had a very nice Christmas. The kids got multiple toys and books. After Christmas, Norman stayed home for two days then we went back to work. The day-to-day life was very simple in Mary's house. We woke up around seven o'clock. We showered, dressed up and went downstairs to eat breakfast when the kids arrived one by one. Then went to the fridge and fixed their breakfast went downstairs, turn on the TV and watch. Mary woke up sometime later and from that point on she was on the telephone until lunch time. After lunch we went shopping, then dinner with Norman, and then sleep.

Before the New Year, Tolstoy Foundation called me. The lady said she had a place for us in St. Joseph, Michigan. Captain, the owner, had a small factory and was looking for an engineer. She asked me when we were returning to the camp. I told her the first days of January. She told me that by that time she was going to have more details. We were all excited about the news and were counting the days when we would return to camp. At Mary's house, we got used to watching TV even though we couldn't understand a word. The kids had their own TV. We watched another one in the living room. It was interesting that Mary's kids never got the measles despite not having the measles before. Finally, Steve's patches disappeared, so we called the doctor at Camp Kilmer who checked out Steve the next day and gave the green light for us to return.

At Camp Kilmer, the lady from Tolstoy made connection with Captain. Since I didn't speak English, I spoke with Marvin who was the warehouse foreman in German. The discussion was unimportant except that I told him that we can leave any time. That same day we received all the papers, airplane tickets, and pocket money from Tolstoy to fly to St. Joseph.

A day later, a small bus took us to a New York downtown hotel. We arrived around 8 o'clock in the evening. We had dinner in the hotel and then walked around the neighborhood. We were a short distance from Times Square. The sidewalk was full of people. We could hardly see the buildings from the neon lights. We didn't go too far from the hotel because we were afraid we were going to get lost.

The next morning, we had breakfast in a Jewish deli, then went to the airport. We flew to Chicago where the Captain was waiting for us. We all fit into his station wagon. The Captain was in his late fifties, he was about six feet tall, dressed in pants and a sweater and spoke with a deep, loud voice. It took us a good four hours to reach St. Joseph. We went through the center of the town then on to a four-lane highway with farmhouses on the side and turned into a driveway and stopped by a two-story farmhouse.

Our First Home

There were lots of cars around the house. Inside, there were probably forty to fifty people. I introduced each of us by first name then carried in all the luggage. We sat down in one room. We met Marvin who started asking questions in German and translating in English. One man was taking lots of photographs of us and this went on for a good hour. We met the Captain's wife and their son, Robert, and Robert's wife, Cindy, who was our neighbor. They took us around the house. Downstairs was the kitchen, the living room, the dining room, the guest room, and the bathroom. Upstairs, there were three bedrooms. The house was sitting on a thirty-acre lot. There was also a large barn and a chicken coop. The house was located next to a four-lane highway. The back side of the thirty acre lot had a small creek.

After a while, people started walking out, and so did the Captain and his wife. Only Robert and Cindy stayed around to show the interior of the house. First one was the thermostat for the heater which was located in a crawl space—pushing hot air through the grills on the floor. And in the crawl space there was a large water heater. There were three window air conditioners, one downstairs and two upstairs. Back in Hungary, there was no house which had temperature-set heater, air conditioner, and full-time hot water. In the beginning, all of us took baths every night until we switched over to showers. We easily got used to the heater and air conditioner, but with the hot water available day and night, that was a pleasure.

On the first day of my job, Marvin (the German speaking foreman) was the only one I could speak to. He introduced me to six or seven people who belonged to his group. I was paired up with one guy and went painting the side of a long hall. During the morning, Marvin came over to where we were working and we went to an office where a young lady, with Marvin helping, type on different papers with my personal information. She told me that I was going to make one dollar and twenty-five cents an hour. We were working five days from Monday through Friday from 8:00 a.m. to 4:30 p.m. with half an hour for lunch and two coffee breaks (ten minutes), one in the morning and one in the afternoon. We would get paid every Friday. If we have overtime, the first two hours are paid 50% more, and if over two hours, 100%.

The group I worked with was a bunch of happy guys with lots of laughs and jokes. Lunchtime was an unending question and answer time. Especially since we were in the local newspaper the first couple of days. The reporter also visited us daily. The Captain had a large office, with lots of books and memorabilia. I was invited the first day in his office to meet his managers. Everybody sat on the carpeted floor around the Captain's desk. Everybody was mostly interested in what I was doing before. I told them my job in the structural steel business. The interest was in the organization of the communist state, the factory, etc. We also discovered that the Captain's wife organized our presence. She bought the house and thirty acres around it six months before our arrival. The house was eighty-two years old and in good shape but did not have a bathroom, or central heating, or air conditioning, and also no furniture or appliances. She got all the appliances, central heating, window air conditioners, and also the bathroom and the plumbing donated from local business because of us. The people working in the factory and offices donated the furniture and filled up the refrigerator. The factory was also new and one day became recognizable with everybody in the town.

The most important people in our life were Robert and Cindy. Robert was a mechanical engineer and his wife was a teacher. Robert was eight years younger than me. Robert worked for his father. Cindy was a housewife. They had a three-year-old daughter. They guided us through the first months of difficulties. Cindy and Maria communicated using a dictionary. Robert was an impatient hand signal pro.

The most important person in the whole group was the Captain. He was a retired Air Force captain who started an engineering business. He dreamt up different projects starting with light assembly work to involved and difficult engineering projects.

My first paycheck was around forty dollars. We went out for a big shopping trip. We had a whole refrigerator full of meat, butter, cooking oil, all kinds of sausage, vegetables, and bread. Not in the fridge were: potato, rice, coffee, etc. We had no problem with any food with picture on the can or box or in clear sacks. We could recognize by sound those food boxes with only names on them by shaking. We filled a whole shopping cart with the stuff we needed and paid ten dollars.

Going from one store to another, everybody recognized us because of the pictures in the newspapers. Some even called us by our first names. It was also common that they bought something for the kids. Mr. Simon, a local postman who spoke Hungarian, provided the transportation but stayed out of the purchasing part. As a reference, we noticed that back in Hungary, we could spend my whole month salary on one week of food. Here, only receiving minimum wage, we needed only 25% of my income, and this is only forty hours of work because there was no overtime. From the point on with overtime, my weekly income was sixty to eighty dollars. Beside food, gasoline was twenty-five cents a gallon, haircut one dollar, a pair of shoes six dollars, and a new car $1600. We paid thirty dollars for the house rent. We were really on the lower end of the pay scale and our standard of living improved many fold. Not speaking about the quality of life and the freedom.

Beside Maria and me, the kids got used to the new life. They really enjoyed the new food, especially fruits. Bananas, oranges, pineapples, were available most of the time. There was also an unbelievable variation of sweet stuffs. Tibor was readily accepted by his schoolmates. They even looked into his mouth to make sure he was the same as they were. At the initial evaluation at school, they accepted him in fourth grade, in math he was two years ahead. Steve and Pat, Cindy's daughter, were a different story.

I don't remember how long both were speaking in his or her own language and perfectly understood each other. Pat was a year older so she ordered Steve around and Steve performed her requests. We watch them playing with toys in the living room for hours without an argument or misunderstanding.

Beside Pat, both Steve and Tibor had matching age friends by the many neighbors. The whole lot was a kid's wonderland. There was a large empty chicken coop and next to that was a good-sized barn with one horse. On the far end, the thirty acres ran into a crystal clear creek. The whole acreage was overgrown with grass.

On the weekend, Robert and Cindy visited. Robert asked if I knew how to drive a car. I said yes. I went upstairs to pick up my Hungarian driver's license. I gave it to Robert, then he said, "Let's go and you drive." He was driving an old pickup truck. I had no problem driving it. Then he said, "Monday we will go and buy a car for you." Then he asked how much cash we had.

Maria said, "Over one hundred dollars."

So Monday morning he picked me up. We went to the police station where I showed them my driver's license which they could not read. Robert mentioned the Captain's name and I received a temporary license. Then we drove to a used car lot. All the cars were covered with more than ten inches of snow. Robert spoke to the owner who picked up a key chain. We all went out to the car lot. With a broom, he cleaned up a car from snow and sat in it (I would bet money that the car wouldn't start), put the key in, and boom the car started. We went back to the office. He said it was a 1949 Ford and it would cost $150 with insurance. I had $145 so Robert gave me five dollars. I sat in the car and drove it to the plant.

We had lots of correspondence with family and friends back in Hungary. We toned down our experience here, as we didn't want to show-off with anything. There were no observations coming back from Hungary concerning our new lifestyle. One friend, seeing the old farmhouse we were living in, did not believe that the two-story house is for one family. The same friend seeing pictures with the four of us with the car told Maria's parents that he restrained himself of commenting on the bunch of lies we wrote to Maria's parents. But being in the United States for six weeks, we saved enough money to buy a car that is too farfetched to believe.

We had the car for two days, when I looked out in the morning and could not believe my eyes. The car was fully covered with snow and the car was nothing more than a bump in the snow. We were living in the east side of Lake Michigan and the cold westerly wind picked up the moisture from the west and covered us in three- to four-feet deep. This happened more than once during every winter.

Spring arrived in late March. Our communication became better every day. It was helped by TV and watching Western movies every night. My hourly rate was raised to one dollar and thirty-seven cents. Also, the Captain hired a Dutch engineer and probably had to balance my salary with his. We met the Dutch guy's family—wife and three kids. Also, we met another Hungarian couple who also came out during the revolution. So slowly, we had a small group of friends.

The spring started out with a new project. Cindy suggested raising chickens since we had a chicken coop. Her suggestion was to raise 124 for the two family.

So they went over to the farm store and ordered 130 baby chickens. All the 130 healthy, yellow, and chirping (nonstop) chickens arrived in two weeks. In two weeks, I cleaned the old chicken coop, fixed any holes on it and fixed the wire fence on the outside run and installed heating lights. The girls picked up soil and sacks of growing mash (with all the nutrition and vitamins the young one needs). The chicken coop had two rooms, a smaller one with sawdust for the baby chicks, and a larger one for grownups with long rods to sit on. The heating light provided nice warmth for the evening that we kept on during the day also, and a dirt floor outside. We were in the business of feeding and providing water every day, making sure that the door was closed for the evening. The surrounding area, and especially the ditch of the creek provided habitat for many unfriendly animals including raccoons, beavers, foxes, etc. We did not have coyotes. For some reason, prey birds never created a problem. Maria and Cindy spent most mornings together. Robert and I drove home for lunch. We also spent most of the weekends together. We also met Cindy's parents and brother, they lived in South Bend.

The Captain was out of town most of the time and so was his secretary. Robert told me that the export business is picking up and that required lots of traveling. I finished my painting assignment and I was transferred to the engineering department mostly working on documentation for the export survey business. Between this and other projects pretty much counted my first year assignment.

The first summer was busy with the outdoor covering, raising the chickens, visiting friends, beach, etc. On the beach, there was a Black beach we didn't understand, but we had no Black friend so it didn't interest us. It took time to get used to eating half raw meat, peanut butter sandwiches with sliced banana, hot dogs with mustard, sliced cucumbers, French fries with ketchup, etc. We loved going to outdoor movies for one dollar for a full carload.

We spent most of the weekends with Cindy's parents at their summerhouse which is an hour drive from us. Cindy had a new baby.

Maria learned to drive. They were occasions which represented the low part of our marriage. She became a very reliable, capable truck driver with the second gear missing.

Gene Bereti was hired by the Captain. He was a Dutch electrical engineer. His father was white but his mother was from the Dutch colonies. Consequently, Gene was considered black in St. Joseph. This presented continuous problems for Gene who was single and wanted to date white girls. He was the most reliable weekly dinner guest. He even visited us when we moved then disappeared and we never heard of him again.

The chickens matured to be processed and frozen. We kept fifteen hens and one rooster for eggs. Maria and Cindy organized an assembly line operation. Cindy picked up one chicken while Maria chopped off the head with an ax. The chickens were running all over the place without a head. Pat and Steve brought the dead chicken into the kitchen. Also, the kids picked up the heads and buried them in a small ditch and covered them up with dirt. The ladies threw the chickens in boiling water, then dumped them in hot wax, removed the feathers, washed them, and put them individually in freezer bags.

Winter arrived and we went over to the next town to visit our Hungarian friends after dinner. When we were ready to leave, we discovered that it was snowing so hard that the visibility was practically zero. The roads were visible, but going home on a two-lane highway with ditches on both sides, it was impossible to see the edges of the road. Maria was going in the center of the road with a flashlight for most of the drive home.

The first Christmas was a memorable, wonderful evening and the houses were decorated with hundreds of lights. We had fresh snow. For Christmas dinner, we cooked carp. Like the tradition in Hungary: the carp was farmed and shipped to Budapest then kept on the Danube River to clean out the mud. It was delicious. We got told that white people don't eat carp, so we bought some other fish. On Christmas evening, there were only four of us. Everybody received many, many gifts. The dinner and the fish and the cookies were traditional Hungarian. We called home and spoke to Maria's parents and my father. The next day we had dinner with Cindy and Robert and their kids. The warmth of the occasion surrounded by peace and freedom was a feeling we never felt in past years.

The year started off with rumors that the Captain was working on a big project for the export business. According to Robert, the new business' main office was going to be in Baghdad.

The winter was brutal again. Spring came fast. Maria and Cindy were back in the chicken business, only Cindy's parents were included in the ritual count, so instead of one hundred twenty-four baby chickens the new number was one hundred eighty chickens. Also there were twenty ducks added to the total. The third farm from us was a large Duck Farm where the girls bought the ducks. I went over with them to pick up the ducks. I don't know how many ducks they processed a day but it was an assembly line operation that went on day and night.

To process the duck, they put the live duck in a funnel with their neck and head hanging down from bottom of the funnel. One person walked before the line of ducks and cut their neck to let the blood out. Then they dumped the ducks in a large round steel container filled with warm, melted wax. After taking them out of the container, they let the wax cool off and harden. Then they removed the wax with all the feathers stuck to the wax then they were cleaned, degutted, and packaged. The owner told me that they cleaned the feathers and sold it and that paid for the overhead operation. The whole process freed me from the concern of killing the ducks because I really loved ducks.

The raising of the ducks in the duck farm was a unique process. There was a great, big, steel building housing all of the ducks. They were separated with wire fences based on their age. Both the water and the food was apportioned and distributed automatically. Only the cleaning and disposing of the soiled sawdust was manual. The sawdust was kept to heat the processing building during winter. The ducks were only disturbed during the evening. After dark every two hours, a buzzer goes off and the lights were turned on for half an hour for feeding and drinking. This shortened their time to reach a certain weight. When I expressed my surprise to the owner, he told me it was an old system. In the new system, the ducks were placed on a wide, long, rubber conveyor band. The conveyor would slowly move all the time. When a duck reached the end of the conveyor, there was a gate. Instead of hitting, they had to walk back and drink and eat in the process. At night the conveyor stopped and lights turned off but restarted every three hours with lights on for half an hour. The rubber belt was washed and scrubbed during the lower position. Our ducks had all the time to grow up and living happily with the chickens.

Maria and Cindy dreamt up a new exercise for Robert and me to keep us awake: a vegetable garden. There was a tennis court size area next to the barn where there were tall weeds growing instead of grass. The ladies thought that this area was previously a vegetable garden. We rented a rototiller and pulverized the whole area to perfection. From that point on we went and bought every small vegetable plant that Noah saved for eternity. After the planting, we discovered that the area was where the previous generation dumped the horse manure. Every vegetable became gigantic, lived forever, and multiplied. We bought forty tomato plants. When the tomato plants became ready to be picked we picked, Cindy picked, and her parents picked. I told the factory that anybody who needed tomatoes to come and pick. Every couple of days I filled a basket with the fallen tomatoes on the ground and gave it to the ducks. They loved it. After a couple of weeks when they saw me coming with the bucket, they ran into the chicken coop.

The summer was perfect. The Captain had a good-sized cabin cruiser that Robert could use for fishing or spending every weekend on Lake Michigan, or barbecuing, swimming, fishing, etc. In the shop, my assignment was pretty much the same.

At home everything was normal.

We went through the whole summer without any excitement. The fall started off where I got told that we were going to be transferred to Baghdad for two years. There weren't any details available. We needed two and a half years to become citizens, and until that point no travel outside the United States, possibly Canada. Baghdad was not the center of tranquility. Any political problem and we could sit with two young boys and wonder about what was going to happen to us. "Sorry we didn't think about that," was not an option.

Not far from our house lived Jeffery—a nice elderly guy in his late fifties whom we met in the plant. He was the Captain's friend and was helping him with all kinds of business issues. He liked to come over to engineering and talk to me about my life under the communists. Around November, he told me he was leaving to Baghdad to organize the main office there for the American personnel and support. When he returned, I was interested to find out what was going on over there. He told me to come over to his house. On the next weekend, I visited him. He said the place is pretty bad. He met an oil mecca millionaire and he invited him to visit him.

Two guys picked up Jeffery with two cars. One had four bodyguards, the other an English speaking servant who sat next to the driver. They went through two little towns then to a road with sand dunes and bare land to a tent city protected on the corner with watchtowers. After arriving to a large, fancy tent, the servant in the car guided Jeffery inside the tent. The boss greeted him, he was interested in the United States, etc. It was followed by a big meal with lots of sweet dishes. Jeffery was hoping that he would get a guided tour of the tent city but it never happened. Instead, Jeffery was driven home the same way he came. Jeffery's opinion was for us to stay in the United States but not to tell our intention to the Captain or his wife until I landed on a new job.

Finally we got the word that we should be ready to leave next year (1959). May, the Captain's secretary, will follow up the paperwork. Robert and Cindy would leave a month earlier.

In the midst of the upcoming activity, one morning, while driving to work, the front of my good old Ford went into a small ditch creating a vibration in the front. The car was pulled into the Ford dealer who concluded the car was not worth the cost of the repair. For $1600 we bought a brand new, light blue 1959 Ford with two doors and a heater and a radio. It was beautiful. Actually the timing was perfect because of my new job, I had to go to Chicago and the old car wouldn't give a good first impression. My first job was to write a resume. Our English reached the maturity that it was generally understood. We still had problems understanding people who spoke with a practically closed mouth. We never had time to attend English classes. Most of our learning came from watching Western movies every night, all night. It was also interesting that people were watching our mouth to help to understand us, but we were not moving our mouth as we were supposed to, so it didn't help. Also if somebody said something that we didn't understand, the person repeated the same thing shouting. We also made mistakes—if somebody didn't get it, we automatically repeated in Hungarian. Robert was the hardest to understand because he spoke really fast with a closed mouth. Naturally, we spoke with an accent. The rule is that if you learn to speak English before the age of fifteen, you could speak without an accent, after that you are a lost cause.

The first interesting job possibility was advertised in the *Popular Mechanics*. A company wanted inventions in the field of games and toys or houseware. It took me two weeks to come up with four simple games. I made a prototype of all of them. The one that I like the most was tennis ball-size rubber ball. The ball was cut in half. In one half, a small parachute was stuffed in that was held to the ball with four strings. If you threw the ball up in the air with the parachute in the ball, the parachute would open up when it would fall down, carrying the unit to a good distance floating in the wind. The other one required balancing two of steel marbles on a round dish starting at the opposite direction to make sure they bump together etc. By the time I was invited for an interview, it was January of 1959. A week before, we drove into Chicago to find the place to make sure I would arrive on time. We had been to Chicago numerous times before with Robert driving. This was the first time I had driven. We found the factory without any problems.

Saturday morning, I woke up early. It was a three and a half hour drive to Chicago. I had an 8 o'clock appointment. When I arrived, I was greeted by a young guy. He was probably my age. I was 37 years old then. After general niceties, I showed him my games. All were demonstrated without any hiccup. He told me he was VP of the company. He made notes of everything we spoke about. He liked the parachute best. He also told me they were making custom injection molded parts. The whole meeting lasted about one hour. I left with mixed feelings. There was no plan to meet again. When I arrived back home, my plan was to increase my effort because I had a deadline middle of April. It was not possible for me to quit my present job and remain in the house and town. All of a sudden, finding a job reached a critical point. We had just sat down for Sunday dinner when the phone rang. The VP called to find out if I could be back in Chicago next Saturday. I asked if I should bring my games, he said no. The president wanted to meet me.

The next week, I met Barry, the president, and his secretary, Barbara. We had a long discussion of my life and my former jobs. When we were done, we went into the next room where he pointed on a good-sized square unit with a rubber hose hanging out of it and said, "This is what I want to make." I asked him what it was, "a dishwasher." It would fit on the kitchen counter next to the kitchen sink and could be attached to the sink faucet. He took the top of it off and there was a garden sprinkler inside of it.

He turned the faucet on, the sprinkler made lots of noise and the water came out from it and into the sink. Then Barry asked if I could design a unit molded from plastic (this one was made from aluminum). I said yes. Then he asked if we can had it under ten dollars. I said I didn't know and would have to make an initial design and then price it out. I had no problem coming up with the design back in St. Joseph but I have no access to prices for the parts. Barry said, "How long will it take you to move to Chicago?"

"We have to find an apartment," I said.

Barry said, "I will hire you." He offered me twelve thousand dollars a year or simply, one thousand dollars a month.

I said, "I have to tell them in St. Joseph that I'm leaving. I don't know what their rules are or how long I have to stay." I thanked Barry that he hired me.

"Call me in the meantime, what is the progress so that I can keep Barry informed," said Barbara.

I drove home with a big smile on my face. When I got home, Maria was interested in all the details. The big news was that our income more than doubled. The big question was how to handle the change. We went over to Robert and Cindy's. They were shocked but happy for us. Robert said "Captain is out of town but I am talking to him every day, let me handle it. Do you want to finish the job at the end of next week?"

"Yes," I said.

The next day, Monday, I went to work waiting on news from Robert. Cindy went over to Maria. Cindy was very happy for us. Her opinion for us to move to Chicago was the right move. Chicago represented lots of opportunities. On Friday, I called Barbara. I told her that I parted ways with the company and Maria and I would spend Saturday looking for apartments.

On Saturday we left for Chicago. We used Cindy's hospitality to help look for home for our two boys. We looked up at least five apartments and not one of them accept kids, especially two boys. We ended up home at 7:00 p.m. The next day, we took the Sunday paper to find lots of addresses for next week.

On Monday morning, I called Barbara and told her the story. "In a week you are going to find something," she said. We were dressing up the kids when the phone rang.

Barbara said, "I told the situation to Barry, Barry has a different solution." They were going to call in the evening. At night Barbara called. She said Barry has a friend who could help us. She gave the information whom to see and suggested to try to see him tomorrow.

I made an appointment the next day. We drove into Chicago the next day. The address was a northwest suburb location. We found the place then located the office. Barry's friend said that he was the builder and he had a number of unsold, empty new homes available.

Barry told him that we should buy one of the larger homes because it was easier to sell. He showed us three different homes, two of them were small ranch homes around twenty thousand dollars. One was a larger bi-level home for twenty-five thousand dollars. The builder said that Barry's wife took care of the down payment. The only thing we had to do was select the color of the rooms and the tiles. After finding the selection, we had to come back and sign the papers by Thursday. Driving home, we couldn't believe what happened. At home we told Cindy and Robert and they couldn't believe it either. For the next three days, we tried to organize all the things we had to do and accomplish. All we had was two hundred dollars in the bank plus the upcoming money for two weeks.

On Thursday, we drove and signed the papers and got told that the closing fee was $800. We told them that we didn't have the money but that we would have it during the weekend. Driving home, we were hoping that Robert could loan us the money. We were wrong but Cindy called her parents and they said they would give us the money. We called Barbara about what was going on (not mentioning that we didn't have the money for the closing fee) and by Monday, we were ready to move.

Monday we drove in to Chicago with the $800. We got told that the house was going to be ready by next weekend. We called Barbara that on the following Monday I could start working. We bought the minimum furniture in St. Joseph on payment. The Captain's wife let us take the dining room table and chairs and the kids' fold out beds. We bought mattresses for ourselves, the kitchen table and chairs, and for the living room, some garden furniture. We bought a washing machine and Cindy loaned us their fridge because they were moving to Baghdad.

Barry sent the company truck to pick up our stuff. It was raining when we arrived to our new home in June of 1959. It was two years and eight months later that we had left our house in Budapest. Starting without a penny, not speaking English, not knowing anybody, having a good job, a good car, and moving into a brand new, tri-level three-bedroom house with all four of us in good health—thank God, and thanks to the United States.